The intercom came on as ALEC popped back to life. "Good news, Crew. We've just emerged from the wormhole!"

"All right," I said. "That was easy."

"And now for the bad news," our computer continued just as cheerfully as before. "Prepare for another crash landing!"

"What was that about easy, Max?" Megan asked.

There wasn't time for me to answer. The train landed so hard that not even Bruno kept his balance. I closed my eyes and waited for the runaway train to stop, one way or the other. When all was quiet again, I could just barely make out voices.

"Listen up!" I whispered excitedly.

Sure enough, we could hear some people in the distance. They were getting louder. We concentrated to hear what they were saying.

"You see, Tony? I told you the Super Crew wouldn't let us down!"

"I didn't believe it possible, but I see it with my own eyes! You were right, Galileo."

We looked at each other wide-eyed. Galileo! We'd made it!

**KINETIC
CITY**
super crew

**Other Books in
The Kinetic City
Super Crew Series**

Bowled Over

The Case of the
Gravity Goof-Up

Chuck Harwood

McGraw-Hill
New York San Francisco Washington, D.C. Auckland Bogotá Caracas
Lisbon London Madrid Mexico City Milan Montreal New Delhi
San Juan Singapore Sydney Tokyo Toronto

McGraw-Hill

A Division of The McGraw·Hill Companies

This novel is a work of fiction. Names, characters, places, and incidents are either the product of the author's imagination or are used fictitiously. Any resemblance to actual events or locales or persons, living or dead, is entirely coincidental.

1 2 3 4 5 6 7 8 9 0 DOC/DOC 9 0 3 2 1 0 9 8

ISBN 0-07-007055-5

The sponsoring editor for this book was Mary Loebig-Giles, the editing supervisor was Penny Linskey, and the production supervisor was Clare B. Stanley. It was set in Century Old Style by Michele M. Zito of McGraw-Hill's Professional Book Group in Hightstown, New Jersey.

Printed and bound by R. R. Donnelley & Sons Company.

McGraw-Hill books are available at special quantity discounts to use as premiums and sales promotions. For more information, please write to the Director of Special Sales, McGraw-Hill, 11 West 19th Street, New York, NY 10011. Or contact your local bookstore.

Contents

About the Crew

It is the near future. Peace has broken out all over the world, and the President of the United States has decided to donate the world's most sophisticated military vehicle, the X-100 Advanced Tactical Vehicle, to "the youth of America, that they might use this powerful tool to learn, to explore, and to help others."

Since the X-100 was designed in a top-secret factory in Kinetic City, the vehicle was renamed **The Kinetic City Express** and the first young crew was dubbed the **Kinetic City Super Crew**.

But who would be the members of the Crew? Kinetic City's mayor, Richard M. Schwindle, puts out a call to the young people of the city. Many answer the call, and seven are chosen: Keisha, Derek, Megan, Curtis, Fernando, PJ, and Max.

Now the Crew travel the world, along with their talkative supercomputer, ALEC, in a tireless quest for truth, justice, and the perfect deep-dish pizza. Their quest may never end.

About the Train

CIA Top Secret Document #113057
DECLASSIFIED: 9/12/99

Originally designed to carry military intelligence teams to trouble spots throughout the world, the X-100 is capable of ultra-high-speed travel, under the control of the Advanced Logic Electronic Computer (ALEC) Series 9000. The vehicle can travel over land on existing train tracks and on tank-style treads. For crossing bodies of water, the X-100 can seal its waterproof bulkheads and travel underwater, using an advanced form of Magneto-Hydrodynamic Drive propulsion. The X-100 has several small vehicles within it which can travel with or without human passengers, including a small submarine and a jet copter. Finally, the X-100 has sophisticated information-gathering capabilities, using 'round-the-clock, high-speed access to the internet, an extensive CD-ROM library, and the ability to generate realistic science simulations in its "Cyber Car."

The Phone Call

"Kinetic City Super Crew, when you want the facts, we hit the tracks, Max dreaming."

"*Ciao*, Maximilian! Galileo here!"

"Galileo? The famous scientist? But I wanted to dream about food."

"Instead you dream about fools, those who want to silence science! Come quickly before it's too late!

CHAPTER ONE

Wormhole!

Kinetic City Express Journal: Bowled Over: The Case of the Gravity Goof-Up. Max reporting.

Okay. I guess I'd better start off by admitting Keisha was right. Two anchovy pizza supremes was one too many. Especially when I was trying to get a last-minute school report done. Keisha warned me that so much food could make me sleepy. She said it might even cause weird dreams. Wow, she didn't know the half of it.

Like I said, I'm Max, the youngest member of the Super Crew and still just in eighth grade. I'm famous for two things. Number one, I can cook like you wouldn't believe. Think of me basically as a famous chef no one's heard of yet. Number two, I sort of exaggerate ff. At least that's what millions of people ___e told me. Okay, well maybe not millions, but still a whole bunch. Anyway, it's not my fault. My imagination was born with a mind of its own.

Which brings me back to those two pizzas and my weird dream. It was all about Galileo, the famous scientist who lived in Italy four hundred years ago. He was the guy I was doing my report on in the first place. As it turned out, I was about to report for duty to help him out of a jam. Keisha would be there, too. And so would Curtis and Megan. For that matter, there'd also be time travel through a wormhole, a caveman named Bruno, and a dungeon full of spiders and rats. But I'm getting ahead of myself. The important point is that this would be no ordinary case. It got off to its bizarre start when the hotline rang deep inside my sleeping brain. Galileo's desperate cry for help jolted me into action ...

"Don't worry, Galileo!" I shouted into the hot-line. "You've called the right place. We'll come to Pisa right away!"

"*Molto grazie*, Maximilian!" he shouted back. His voice was distant and the static made it hard to hear. "I knew I could count on the Super . . ."

The line went dead. It's tough to get a good connection to someone who lived four centuries ago. I didn't have time to worry about it, though. I needed to find the others and tell them what was up. As it turned out, I didn't have to. Keisha found me. The Kitchen Car doors *whooshed* open and she came running in.

"Max! You've got to get to the Control Car! Something really strange is going on!"

I'd never seen Keisha look so scared. Ever. Normally she's the cool, leader-of-the-pack type.

"What's up?" I asked. I was sure it couldn't be stranger than Galileo's phone call.

"The train's been sucked into another dimension! I think it's a wormhole!"

Of course, I could always be wrong.

"C'mon! Curtis and Megan need our help!"

I joined Keisha and we ran toward the Control Car. It didn't take long to realize the word 'strange' didn't quite cut it. The entire train was spinning through what looked like an endless tunnel of pure energy. Freaky, multicolored lights wrapped around the train's windows like a tube. It was hard to describe. Try to imagine a bunch of Christmas tree lights spinning around in a dryer. Now imagine that you're stuffed inside the dryer, too. See what I mean? Weird.

As we ran inside the Control Car, Megan and Curtis were already there. Neither of them looked very happy.

"Anything to report, Crew?" Keisha asked, trying to sound brave.

Megan stood at the control panel. Her eyes were wide and the weird light coming through the windows made her face look strange. She had been hunched over the keyboards and switches, desperately trying to bring ALEC the computer to life.

"Megan," Keisha repeated louder. "Is there anything new to report?"

"Huh?" Megan glanced up and noticed us. "This wormhole thinga-ma-jiggy's messing up ALEC! The last report I got from him said we were about to go backwards in time."

Keisha tried to stay cool. "Anything else?"

"Yeah," Megan said, wiping some sweat off her forehead. "We're doomed."

"Can't anybody be optimistic around here?" Keisha was starting to sound a little nervous herself. "Curtis? How 'bout you?"

Curtis sat on the floor with his back to the wall. He looked totally depressed. "And the worst thing about it all," he said as if the question had caught him in mid-thought, "is that I just finished the Boom-Bot, my coolest invention ever."

He pointed glumly to the thing sitting beside him. It looked like a miniature portable stereo mounted on little tank treads.

"What's that?" I asked.

"It's a miniature portable stereo mounted on little tank treads."

"Oh . . . neat," I said, not sure if I sounded all that convincing.

"I pieced it together from spare parts lying around the Lab Car," Curtis continued, half talking to himself. "It was going to be my breakthrough invention."

"What's it do?" I asked.

"Lets you cruise through life with your own movie soundtrack. Here, I'll show you."

He stood up, pulled a remote control from his jacket pocket and punched in some numbers. The Boom-Bot spun on its little treads as it followed him across the floor, cranking out music. *Yesterday, all my troubles seemed so far away. Now it looks as though they're here to stay. Oh, I believe, in yesterday.*

"Hey, the Beatles," Keisha said with a grin. "We must be passing back through the 1960s about now."

"I think my mom left one of her CDs in the boom box," Curtis said.

"Curtis, would you please turn that thing off?" Megan pleaded. "We're in the middle of a life or death situation here."

Curtis punched another button on the remote.

Help! I need somebody! Help! Not just anybody! Heeelllppp!

Megan put her hands on her hips, tapped her foot and glared. Curtis turned the Boom-Bot off. "Sorry, Megan," he said sadly. "But we might as well face the music. We're goners."

"What do you mean, we're goners?" I shouted, losing my cool for a second. "We can't be goners! I've got a school report due tomorrow and I still haven't fed the dog, or taken out the trash, or cleaned my room, or . . . or . . ." I stopped when I realized the others were just shaking their heads and staring at me.

"Okay, everybody," Keisha said, trying to keep calm. "Let's not lose our grip here. How did the KC Express get into this mess in the first place?"

Megan stopped her useless typing at ALEC's keyboard. "It all started when I hit a switch on the control panel for automatic pizza delivery."

Keisha looked confused. "What switch for automatic pizza delivery?"

Megan pointed at a little silver knob poking up from the middle of the control panel. Funny. None of us had ever noticed it there before. Keisha walked over and took a look.

"Megan," she said, "this doesn't say 'Automatic Pizza Delivery.' It says 'Automatic *Pisa* Delivery.' "

The word 'Pisa' triggered my memory of Galileo's phone call.

"Uh oh . . ." I said. The Crew turned and looked at me again.

"What do you mean by, 'uh oh', Max?" Keisha asked slowly.

"This whole wormhole thing is part of our next case," I answered. "We just got a call from Galileo on the hotline."

Curtis slowly raised his hand. "Um, Max . . . you don't mean Galileo the famous scientist, do you?"

I nodded my head. "Yep. That's the one. He needs us in Pisa to help him figure out what's gone wrong with a big experiment."

Keisha shook her head. "Max, how could he possibly call us? He lived four centuries ago."

"He's the guy I was doing my report on when I fell asleep."

"So?" Megan asked. "What does that have to do with this?"

"Dont'cha see?" I said. "We're stuck inside one of my dreams."

You could have heard a pin drop. At least until Curtis let out a groan. The Crew didn't much appreciate being stuck inside my imagination. Don't ask me why.

"Wake up, Max!" Curtis shouted.

I shrugged my shoulders. "Sorry, Curtis. You can't wake me up from inside the dream. Only someone in the real world can do that."

"Oh, great," Megan said sarcastically. "So now we're stuck here until someone finds you snoring on top of the table."

"That's not true," I said in self-defense. "I'm snoring *under* the table."

Megan folded her arms. "Whatever."

Keisha stepped between us before an argument broke out. "C'mon, Crew, we're trapped in Max's mind so we might as well make the best of it."

Curtis looked out the window. "Hey! There's something at the end of the tunnel!"

"What is it, Max?" Megan frowned. "Another train?"

"How should I know?"

"It's your dream."

"So? My imagination has a . . ."

Megan finished my sentence for me. "I know. I know. A mind of its own."

Keisha had pressed her face to the glass. "Well, whatever it is, it's definitely getting closer."

I looked out the Control Car's super-reinforced windshield. Sure enough, at the end of the pipeline of swirling lights, there was a single white light about the size of a marble held at arm's length. I watched it grow. Soon it was the size of a baseball. Then a basketball. Then . . .

"Uh oh," I said again, only this time with even more of a sinking feeling.

"Take cover!" Megan shouted. "We're going to crash!"

Teamwork in a crisis is what we're best at. In this case, our teamwork consisted of a group scream. A nice long, loud one.

CHAPTER TWO

Early Birds

'Crash' wasn't exactly the right word for it. It was more like a thud. Like being in the back of a speeding school bus when it rolls over a big pothole. Not exactly life-threatening, but still hard enough to knock you around. At least that's what happened to Curtis, Megan, and me. In less than an eye blink, the swirling colors of the wormhole switched to sunlight and we were on our butts. Only Keisha, a track champ, was athletic enough to keep from falling down ...

For a moment, no one spoke. I could hear song-birds. Lots and lots of them.

"Is . . . is everybody all right?" It was Keisha. She sounded worried that none of us had moved yet.

Megan and I answered at the same time. "I'm okay." "Ditto."

"Curtis?" Keisha continued. "How about you?"

Curtis sat up and gave himself a quick once-over. "No blood, no foul."

"Can you guys stand up?"

We could. I wiped the dust off the backside of my jeans and looked out the Control Car's windshield. It wasn't hard to figure out where all the bird songs were coming from. We were in the middle of a forest. A big, green, thick one.

"Uh oh," Megan whispered behind me. "I don't think we're in Kinetic City anymore."

Curtis sighed when he looked out the window. He's not a big fan of the wild. "A forest. Why did it have to be a forest? Why couldn't we land in civilization? Or at least a strip mall?"

"Um, Megan," Keisha suggested slowly. "Why don't you see if we can get ALEC now?"

"Check," she replied, trying not to sound scared.

I pressed my nose against the glass for a better look. It was light outside, but the sun wasn't above the trees.

Keisha stood beside me. "It's either dawn or dusk," she commented. "It's hard to tell."

Curtis didn't like looking out the window. He turned away to see if his Boom-Bot was okay. It was. At least judging by the Beatles music that suddenly filled the air. *Hey, Jude, don't make it bad. Take a sad song and make it better!*

"Hey, Curtis . . ." It was Megan. "Could you turn that android jukebox down? ALEC's coming back to life!"

Sure enough, I heard the familiar beeps and pings of our supercomputer revving up. We all breathed a big sigh of relief. No matter how tight a fix we might be in, if ALEC was working, everything would turn out all right.

"Heeelllooo, Crew, did you know my sensors are detecting ambient carbon dioxide at Pleistocene levels? If I didn't know any better, I'd say we've traveled roughly 40,000 years back in time."

The Crew let out a fresh round of groans.

"Any ideas on how that might have happened?" ALEC asked.

"I hit the automatic delivery switch a bunch of times and launched us too far back in time," Megan admitted. Not that her explanation helped much.

"I'm afraid I don't understand what you're talking about," our computer admitted.

"We're trapped in one of my dreams," I answered.

"Oh," ALEC said. "I guess that explains those chickens jazzercising in the Gym Car."

"What?" Curtis practically choked in disbelief.

"Behold security monitor number three, Crew." ALEC replied, switching it on automatically. We looked up at the row of screens that lined the wall along the ceiling. Our jaws dropped. Five chickens in tight pink spandex were leaning against the wall and breathing hard.

"They've stopped," I said.

Keisha broke out laughing. "I guess their

cluck just ran out."

The rest of us ignored her pun. Curtis tapped me on the shoulder. "Max . . ."

"Yeah?"

"You should think about donating your brain to science. Immediately."

ALEC switched off the security monitor. "Perhaps you'd better tell me all you know," he suggested.

I tried my best. It wasn't easy. ALEC's built for logic and this whole mess was anything but logical. "It all started when I got a call from Galileo."

"The famous scientist who lived from 1564 to 1642?"

"Right."

A pause. A beep or two. Then . . . "I see."

"Yeah," I continued, too excited to worry about what ALEC thought of my mental grip. "Only when I took the call in the Kitchen Car, I didn't know an Automatic Pisa Delivery Switch had appeared in the Control Car at the same time."

"Of course," our computer confirmed. "How could you?"

"Exactly. And Megan wasn't paying close attention and mistook 'Pisa' for 'Pizza.'"

"A common human mistake," ALEC said.

"Yeah," I said. "And the more she flicked the switch, the further back the wormhole took us."

"Aha!" ALEC said. "A wormhole is a sort of tunnel in the space-time continuum that acts like a shortcut from one place and time to another. It can have very tricky physics, you know."

"Tell us about it," Megan muttered under her breath.

"Where are we, anyway?" Keisha asked.

"Hold on," ALEC said. "By correlating the still visible stars and planets to their apparent position in the Upper Pleistocene, I can do a positional check and determine our exact coordinates."

I cocked my head from side to side. I wasn't quite sure what that meant. I wasn't the only one.

"Whatever, ALEC," Megan said. "Just tell us where we are."

"Checking!" For the next few moments, ALEC's beeps drowned out all the song birds. Then came the DING!

"Coordinates determined, Crew!" he announced proudly. "We're at 43.5 degrees north and 10.5 degrees west."

"Uh huh. So where's that?" Curtis asked.

"The exact site of the modern-day city of Pisa, Italy."

Megan rolled her eyes. "Great. So we're here. Now all we gotta do is wait forty thousand years. Anyone bring a deck of cards?"

"I can reroute us through the wormhole to the Pisa of Galileo's time," ALEC continued. "But it's going to take a while for me to figure out the physics. Please excuse me while I go into hyper-mode."

And with that, ALEC was gone. He was still on, but when he was in hyper-mode, all his available circuits were focused on one problem only. For a while at least, we were back on our own. As it turned out, the timing was pretty bad.

"Uh oh . . ." I said, still looking out the window.

"You keep saying that," Megan observed nervously. "And each time it's something worse."

"What is it, Max?" Keisha asked.

I was so shocked I couldn't answer. I could only point out the window.

"What?" Megan asked, sounding a little annoyed. "The stream?"

"Up higher."

"The butterflies?" Keisha guessed.

"Down lower."

"The cavemen!" Curtis shouted.

"Oh my gosh," Keisha gasped. "They're coming toward us!"

I counted them as they crossed the shallow stream. Five. Seven. Ten. A dozen all together. Each one armed with a huge stone ax. They fanned out like a wolf pack and moved toward the Control Car in a low, slow crouch.

"What's that they're wearing?" I asked.

"Pieces of fur sewn together," Curtis replied.

Keisha wrinkled her nose. "Fur is so nasty."

Megan turned to look at her. "We're forty thousand years back in time, Keisha. What do you expect them to wear, polyester?"

"Good point."

"Check out those horns on the leader's head," Curtis said. "I think those are elk antlers."

When the group got about a hundred feet from the train, everyone but the one with the antlers stopped in his tracks. As he came closer, we could see that he wore a necklace of raven heads. They looked really fresh. It was hard not to stare. It was hard not to look away.

"If that guy asks me to the prom," Megan joked nervously, "I'm saying I already have a date."

But he didn't look like he was going to ask us anything, not with his weapon raised over his head.

"I hope our bullet-proof glass is ax-proof, too!" Curtis gulped.

The guy didn't clobber our train though. Instead, he just yelled something, shook the ax around, and then touched the windshield with his fingertips. I squinted at the oily smudges he left behind. "Hey, real caveman fingerprints."

"He probably forgot to wash his hands after his last mammoth burger," Megan observed.

The smudges were nothing compared to what came next. The guy dipped his hand in a small pouch at his side and then pressed it back to the glass. This time it left a big green hand print.

"Hey!" Megan shouted. "Elk boy just made graffiti on our train! Of all the nerve!"

"Hold on, Megan," Curtis said, "I think he just gave us a stamp of approval. Look!"

We did. It was kind of weird. As soon as the leader left his mark, all the other cavemen dropped their clubs and bowed down toward the train.

"Check it out," Curtis continued. "They think we're some kind of gods."

"I guess that makes sense," Megan said. "How often does a supertrain come rolling through this neck of the woods?"

"Aww," Keisha said, noticing that one of the cavemen had a yellow flower in his hair over one ear. "I betcha they're not so mean after all."

"I think you're right," I agreed. "I'm gonna try and communicate with them."

Megan looked at me as if I had gone fully nuts. "What? You gonna ask 'em in for tea?"

"Look," I said, not backing down. "Just because they're different from us doesn't mean we can't be friends."

Megan still looked skeptical.

"Besides," I continued. "It's *my* dream and I want some adventure."

Before anyone had a chance to disagree, I hit the green button on the wall and opened up the Control Car's door to the outside.

I was prepared for the cavemen's looks. Their smell, though, was another issue entirely.

"*Whewf,*" Curtis said, holding his nose. "Don't tell me, let me guess. Deodorant hasn't been invented yet."

I had to admit, I hadn't smelled anything worse since the time my family came back from summer vacation and our freezer had broken. You do not want to know what defrosted chicken smells like after two weeks. Still, personal hygiene aside, I thought it was important we make contact. After all, we were ambassadors from the future.

"We come in peace," I shouted as Keisha stood at my side. Curtis and Megan kept squarely behind us.

The guy with the antlers took a couple of steps back, but his eleven buddies grabbed their axes and came up closer to join him. They stood in a big bunch less than ten feet away.

"Hey, they must've been out hunting rabbits," I heard Curtis comment from behind.

It was true. They did have a lot of rabbits. Half of them had at least four or five hanging from the thin leather straps they used for belts.

It gave me an idea of how to win their trust. I'd appeal to their stomachs in the timeless language of a well-cooked meal.

"So, um, are you guys hungry?" I asked.

No response. I tried again.

"You don't have to eat those rabbits raw, you know."

Still no response.

"Um . . . forty thousand and thirty years from now I'm going to be a world-famous chef."

They edged a little closer to the train. Maybe just five feet away now. I was getting through to them!

"That's right. In fact, I already know an unbelievable recipe for rabbit fricassee."

They looked at each other and grunted some more. I couldn't tell if it was about the fricassee.

"Max, English hasn't been invented yet," Keisha said. "Try sign language."

I did just that. I pointed at the rabbits and then pretended like I was cooking them in a skillet. They smiled. One even laughed with a loud snort.

"Keep going, Max," Megan encouraged. "You got 'em laughing!"

I pretended like I was eating and rubbed my belly in satisfaction. That got them laughing even louder.

"Keep going, Max," Curtis shouted. "They love you."

I grinned and gave the Neanderthals a big thumbs-up sign. Big mistake. Their laughter stopped as suddenly as if I had just poked them all in the eye. They raised their axes and charged!

"Close the door!" Keisha shouted.

I hit the 'lock' button. Too late. The guy with the antlers was able to jump aboard. Luckily, the flashing lights from our control panel caught him completely off guard. As his eyes adjusted to the light, Megan came up with a brilliant plan.

"Run!"

See what I mean? Genius just doesn't get any better than that.

CHAPTER THREE

A Perfect Strike

Now I've been around long enough to know
that life is full of all kinds of frightening
stuff: tornadoes, house fires, school bullies, big
dogs foaming at the mouth. But nothing had
prepared me for this—an ax-swinging caveman
hot on our heels. We bolted through the train
with doors swooshing open and closed as fast
as we could run through them. But the caveman
was fast too, and he finally caught up to us in
the very last section of the KC Express, the
Bowling Car...

"Oh no!" I shouted as we reached the bowling
pins. "The end of the lane!"

Megan stamped her foot in the gutter.
"We're pinned!"

Wow. We must have been really scared. Two puns in a row and Keisha hadn't even laughed.

"Do . . . do you think he saw us come in here?" Curtis said, nearly tripping over his Boom-Bot. He had taken off running with the remote still in his hand and the robot had automatically tagged along.

The sliding door *shwooshed* back open and the big, beefy caveman stormed in.

Keisha nodded her head. "Yep."

Megan was the first to react. She picked up one of the bowling pins and shook it around. "Okay! That's far enough, Buster! No one in here without goofy shoes."

"*Grraaag!*"

Megan screamed, dropped the pin, and ducked behind us.

Not that we could be much help. We stood like pins as the caveman lumbered toward us, two hundred and fifty pounds of hairy nightmare about to bowl us over. Time for desperate measures.

"Quick, Curtis," Keisha whispered. "Use your Boom-Bot!"

Curtis looked at her like she was nuts. "Are you kidding? It's made for dancing. Not for fighting."

"That's my point," Keisha replied. "Blast 'em with the music!"

His hands shaking, Curtis grabbed the remote and triggered the music full volume. *She loves you yeah! yeah! yeah! She loves you yeah! yeah! yeah!*

The caveman's eyes grew wide and he stopped in his tracks. The Boom-Bot had definitely confused him.

"Charge him with it!" Keisha shouted.

Curtis pushed some more buttons on his remote and the Boom-Bot went tearing up the lane. This time it was the caveman's turn to scream.

"Aaaii!"

He leapt behind a rack of bowling balls and howled like a wolf as the Boom-Bot circled round. All the noise was hard on our ears. Still, it was a lot better than getting slugged in the head with an ax.

"That was the most terrifying moment of my life," Curtis gasped.

I nodded. My knees were shaking so much they were actually knocking together.

"That ax is still a headache waiting to happen," Megan said nervously.

"Check," Keisha agreed. "One of us needs to take it away."

She glanced at us. No one volunteered. "Oh, all right," she said. "I'll get it."

Keisha walked toward the caveman very carefully, like she was approaching a big stray dog. It wasn't a problem though. The Boom-Bot had totally freaked him out. As she got closer, he put his hands over his eyes and made a long, sad wail. "*Aaarrruuu!*"

"Aw, it's okay," I heard Keisha say over the music. "We're not going to hurt you."

The big guy didn't seem to buy it. "*Aaarrruuu!*"

"Hey," Megan called out from behind me.

"He sounds just like Bruno."

"Who's Bruno?" I asked.

"My neighbor's Siberian Husky."

"*Aaarrruuu!*"

I had to admit, the caveman did sound like a big wolf howling at the moon. Not that it intimidated Keisha. She grabbed the ax very slowly and then stuck it in the little closet where we keep the bowling shoes. 'Bruno' hardly noticed her at all. He just sat there looking miserable.

"Great. So we got the ax," Megan observed. "But now what? We're still stuck forty thousand years back in time."

There was a brief, high-pitched whine as the KC Express's intercom came on. ALEC was finished with his hyper mode. "Heelllooo, Crew! My sensors have been looking for you all over the train. In a few seconds, we'll re-enter the wormhole and head straight for Galileo's Ital . . ." ALEC stopped himself mid-sentence. His video camera must have picked up our visitor. "Oh. Did you know that there's a

Neanderthal on board? They were a species of powerfully built humans who once inhabited large parts of Europe and Western Asia but are now extinct."

"This one sure isn't extinct," Megan pointed out. But ALEC was no longer listening. He couldn't. His circuits were swarmed as the wormhole swallowed us back up. I could see the rainbow-colored lights flashing past the Bowling Car's porthole windows. Bruno could, too. It just made him howl even louder. *"Aaarrruuu!"*

The wormhole also affected the Boom-Bot. The loud music became a loud static. Keisha bent over and turned it off. "Hey, Curtis, looks like you'll have to go back to the drawing board if you want to make your Boom-Bot wormhole-proof."

No answer.

"Curtis?" Keisha repeated.

Still no answer. We all looked around. Nothing.

"He's gone," Megan said.

"Gone, but not forgotten," I said with a grin.

Keisha looked down at me. "What are you talking about, Max?"

I only smiled wider. "You'll see. My dream just sent him on an important mission. He'll be back in a jiffy."

"Why don't you send me off on an important mission?" Megan said. "Like to a beach on Hawaii."

I shook my head. "Sorry, Megan. I can't control things like that. I can only tell you what's going on at the moment."

"Okay, Mr. Announcer," Keisha said. "So what's going on now?"

I kept my big grin. "We teach Bruno how to bowl, of course!"

CHAPTER FOUR

Pisa Delivery At Last

I had one good reason for wanting to teach Bruno how to bowl: caveman control. If we could point his violent instincts toward the pins instead of toward us, we would stand a much better chance of keeping my dream adventure from becoming a nightmare. In the end, things worked out better than I could have imagined . . . um, so to speak. Not only did Bruno take to bowling like an eggroll to duck sauce, but the whole process ended up making us a new friend. The ice-breaking sure made me nervous though...

"Um . . . Mr. Caveman?"

No response. I was slowly walking up the

lane. Keisha and Megan were still crouched along the back wall. I had to solve this mess solo.

"Mr. Caveman? . . . Sir?"

He looked up from the scoring table where he sat and let out a low growl. Not exactly the response I was looking for.

"Um . . . you wanna try something fun?"

He snorted. Call me an optimist, but I took that for a 'yes.'

"It's called bowling."

He glowered at me as I reached the ball rack. I picked up the biggest one. A sixteen pounder.

"*Graaak!*" He jumped to his feet so fast I nearly dropped the ball on my foot.

"Careful, Max," Keisha shouted. "He thinks you're trying to attack him."

I glanced at Bruno's massive thighs and chest and thought about my own inability to do a single pull-up. "You've gotta be kidding."

"Who knows?" Megan said. "Just show him how it's done first."

It was as good a plan as any. "Okay, Bruno," I tried to sound as cheerful as possible. "Watch me have some fun here."

I turned and rolled the sixteen pounder down the lane. Gutter ball. Megan was the first to comment.

"Good going, Max. One more like that and he'll wanna join a league."

"Hey, gimme a break. That ball was heavy."

Bruno growled again. He was so close I could smell his armpits. It made my eyes water.

"Hurry, Max," Keisha urged. "Try one you're used to."

I picked up one of the ten pounders. As luck would have it, it was the same ball I had used to bowl my first one hundred game the week before. I launched it down the lane. A seven / ten split. Figured. My one big chance to break through to the caveman and I'd blown it. But that's when something cool happened. Bruno laughed. Not just the 'he-he-he' kind. But the loud, gasping-belly yucks of someone who can't get enough air.

"Hey," I said, my eyebrows furrowing. "What's so funny about a seven / ten split?"

"Don't worry about it, Max," Keisha said. "The important thing is that you got him laughing."

"Right," Megan agreed. "Now watch me spare us all."

She picked up a bowling ball and rolled it down the lane. It clipped the ten pin on the side and sent it flying into the seven, knocking it over as well. Bruno rolled on the floor and howled with laughter.

"See if he wants to try," Keisha suggested.

I waited for the machine to reset the pins and then, very carefully, handed a bowling ball to Bruno. He ignored the finger holes and grabbed it like a baseball. Then, taking half a step forward, he whipped it sidearm with a quick flick of his thick wrist. The bowling ball flew over the lane and smacked into the pins half a foot off the ground. A perfect strike!

"Whoa!" all three of us said pretty much at the same time.

The door flew open and Curtis walked in to find our eyes wide and Bruno bent over double, laughing his head off.

"What's up?" he asked.

"Watch this," Keisha said.

The pin resetter moved away and Bruno grabbed another bowling ball. Again he threw it sidearm. Again it smashed into the pins without so much as touching the floor. Another strike.

"Whoa!" Curtis said. "Is that legal?"

"Who cares?" I said. "He's a natural."

Bruno giggled like a giant kid.

Curtis looked at me. "It was good thinking dreaming me to the Supply Car like that, Max. I was able to make a little present for our guest. Look."

He held up a bunch of air fresheners tied together by a thick piece of yellow yarn. They were those tree-shaped kind you see hanging in cars.

"Lovely," Megan said. "Now he'll just have to wait a few thousand years for the rearview mirror to be invented."

Curtis shook his head. "No, it's for him to wear. It's a necklace."

I waved my hand under my nose. Bruno was working up a cavemanly sweat. "That might not be a bad idea. See if he likes it."

The caveman had just picked up another bowling ball and was waiting impatiently for the pin rack to clear. Curtis tapped him on the shoulder in genuine respect. "Bruno, in honor of your superhuman bowling, I give you this, a necklace of air fresheners."

Bruno didn't understand a word, but that didn't stop his eyes from getting a little misty. From his expression it was obvious the necklace was one of the most beautiful things he had ever seen. "*Rungba!*" he gasped. Whatever that meant.

"Yeah, *rungba*," Curtis said, slipping the necklace over Bruno's extra thick neck.

"Whew," I said. "It's a lot fresher in here already."

Curtis began to move back toward us, but Bruno reached out and caught him on the arm.

"*Rungba!*" he said, taking off his raven-head necklace and offering it to Curtis.

"Uh . . . no thanks," he said. "You keep it, Bruno."

Bruno scowled angrily. "*Rungba! Rungba!*"

"Um, Curtis," Keisha said carefully, "for the sake of our continued good health, I think you'd better put that on."

"Yeah," Megan said, nodding her head. "*Rungba* must mean some kind of peace trade."

What could Curtis do? It was either put it on or make Bruno mad. Real mad. He closed his eyes and slipped it on. Megan was the first to comment. "Stylin', Curtis. *Very* stylin.' "

"Yeah," Keisha laughed. "I give it raven reviews."

"Hah, hah," Curtis replied, looking pretty queasy.

The intercom came on as ALEC popped back to life. "Good news, Crew. We've just emerged from the wormhole!"

"All right," I said. "That was easy."

"And now for the bad news," our computer

43

continued just as cheerfully as before. "Prepare for another crash landing!"

"What was that about easy, Max?" Megan asked.

There wasn't time for me to answer. The train landed so hard that not even Bruno kept his balance. I closed my eyes and waited for the runaway train to stop, one way or the other. When all was quiet again, I could just barely make out voices.

"Listen up!" I whispered excitedly.

Sure enough, we could hear some people in the distance. They were getting louder. We concentrated to hear what they were saying.

"You see, Tony? I told you the Super Crew wouldn't let us down!"

"I didn't believe it possible, but I see it with my own eyes! You were right, Galileo."

We looked at each other wide-eyed. Galileo! We'd made it!

"Wow!" I gasped, hopping up and looking out the window. It was pretty dark outside, but I could see two men heading toward the train.

"We're actually here!"

"Well, don't just stand there, Max," Keisha said. "Open the door."

I hit the switch to the outside hatch and we all jumped out. The train had come to a stop in the middle of a huge green lawn just on the outskirts of Pisa. It was the famous *Campo dei Miracoli*, the Square of Miracles. We took a quick look around. Daylight was just breaking, and in the gray light we could see that to our right was a big cathedral. To our left the famous Leaning Tower. In front of us, about as far away as second base is to home plate, there was a big stone wall. Behind it we could see the rooftops of the town of Pisa itself. There wasn't a car, billboard, or telephone pole in sight. We were back in the year 1601!

"Freaky," Megan said, summing up the strangeness for the rest of us. "Now I know how Alice in Wonderland must have felt."

We stood and watched as the two men ran the last little bit to the train. The older one was tall with a long, brown beard and puffy hat that looked like a couch pillow on his head. That, I assumed, was Galileo. The shorter man wasn't much older than Keisha. He had dark peach fuzz on his cheeks and was wearing a simple brown robe with a large red 'T' sewn over the chest.

I bowed low. "Galileo, I presume?"

"*Buon giorno e molto grazie*," the great scientist boomed. "Good morning and many thanks for coming!"

We all smiled from ear to ear. You know how you can meet someone for the first time and instantly know you're going to like them? Galileo was like that for us. His eyes didn't just shine, they sparkled. And, when he spoke, his hands darted around like they were conducting some invisible orchestra. Bruno, however, seemed more interested in Galileo's big puffy hat. He reached out to touch it, but Megan gently slapped him on the wrist. "Stop that. You already have some very nice elk antlers of your own."

Bruno pulled his hand back and pouted. Galileo straightened his hat, did a double-take at Curtis's raven-head necklace, and then introduced the other man.

"This is my teaching assistant," he said in his thick Italian accent, "Tony Biagagga de Arivaderchioli."

"Hi, Mr. Biagagga de Arivaderchioli," I tried to say.

"Please, just call me Tony."

Galileo's assistant seemed nice enough though his breath was almost as strong as Bruno's armpits.

Galileo looked at me. "Are you Maximilian?"

"That's right," I said. Then I gestured to the Crew. "And this is Megan, Keisha, and Curtis."

"And your furry companion?" Galileo said, glancing over at Bruno.

"That's Bruno," I explained. "He's just along for the ride."

"I see," Galileo said. "Well, Maximilian, I must say you command a fine-looking group!"

"Command?" Megan repeated, not sure if she had heard correctly. "Did I miss a meeting or something?"

"We don't have a commander, Galileo," I quickly explained. "We work as a team."

Galileo only raised an eyebrow and smiled, but Tony jerked back in surprise. "You don't have a commander?" he asked in confusion. "Who tells you what to do?"

Galileo made a tut-tut sound and shook his finger at his assistant. "Not so fast, Tony. The ways of the future can be different from the ways of the past. Remember what the Renaissance just taught us?"

Tony scratched his peach fuzz and thought about it. "Um . . . Chew with your mouth closed?"

Galileo looked annoyed. "Yes, yes. And what else?"

Tony tried to look like he was in deep thought or something. It was obvious he didn't have the slightest. Galileo had to fill him in. Personally, I was glad he did. I was a little weak on the whole Renaissance thing myself.

"The Renaissance began on Italian soil in the fourteenth century," Galileo explained. "While it marked the 'rebirth' of classical art, architecture, and literature, its greatest promise was that we humans can use our powerful minds to understand the world around us!"

"Oh yeah," Tony said. "That's right. I forgot."

But Galileo didn't hear him. He was on a total roll. "We live at the beginning of the Modern Age, Tony," he thundered, his hands fluttering around like moths. "Think of the possibilities! Through careful observation of experiments, we can know the secrets of Nature herself! Behold! We live at the dawn of the New Science!"

Tony looked like he might faint. "You . . . you are *so* smart, Galileo."

But Galileo's friendly face suddenly looked very serious. "Super Crew, you have arrived at a moment of great peril."

"Oh wonderful," Curtis griped under his breath.

"I have powerful enemies," Galileo said, keeping his voice low.

"You do?" Keisha asked. "Who?"

"Walk with me over to the Leaning Tower. I'll explain. Tony, go on ahead and unveil the ramp."

The teaching assistant bowed low. "Shall I crawl there on my hands and knees, master?"

Galileo shook his head. "No, no. Just walk."

"Shall I walk backwards?"

"No, just walk normally."

"But then I won't be able to gaze upon your genius."

Galileo sighed. "We'll be coming along right behind you."

"Promise?"

Galileo nodded. "Promise."

Tony beamed from ear to ear. "Then I obey at once!"

He wheeled around and lumbered off in the direction of the Leaning Tower. When Galileo was sure he was out of earshot, he filled us in on what was up. "I wanted to talk to you privately, Crew."

"What's up?" Keisha asked, her voice low.

Galileo stopped in his tracks and looked around nervously. He motioned at Bruno with his eyes. "What about the big one? Can he be trusted?"

"Don't worry, Galileo," I said. "Bruno won't tell anybody anything."

Galileo began his explanation. "You see, Super Crew, there are powerful forces who would like nothing more than to silence me and the New Science for good!"

"There are?" Megan asked. "Who?"

Galileo's voice dropped and his eyes narrowed to two thin slits. "The Inquisition!"

I'm sure it was only a coincidence, but just as Galileo spoke, a low roll of thunder rumbled off in the distance. I gulped. "Who . . . who's the Inquisition?"

"Narrow-minded men who are afraid of learning anything new," Galileo replied. "When it comes to subjects like physics, they are blind followers of Aristotle."

"Who's Aristotle?" I asked.

"A philosopher who lived in ancient Greece. He was a brilliant man, but much of his work in physics is just plain . . ." Galileo stopped himself before a bad word slipped out. Megan finished his sentence.

"Plain hooey?"

Galileo nodded. "*Hooeyismo.*"

"So the Inquisition doesn't want you to prove that Aristotle's physics were wrong, huh?" Curtis said.

"Exactly," Galileo confirmed. "The Inquisition is against learning anything new. It's as if the Renaissance never happened!"

"Relax, Galileo," I said, trying to calm him down. "We'll do whatever it takes to get your experiment back on track."

Galileo looked at us with hope in his eyes. "Excellent, that's just what I needed to hear. Come! Let me show you my acceleration ramp. A simple experiment that will really get the New Science rolling!"

CHAPTER FIVE

Ramping Up

Meeting Galileo made the whole trip through the wormhole worthwhile. From his big smile and even bigger ideas we could tell he was still a kid at heart. Obviously we wanted to do whatever we could to help. But just who were these guys he called the Inquisition? Would they make life dangerous for us for trying to lend a hand? As we would soon learn, the short answer to that question was a big fat 'yes'!

As the day quickly grew lighter, we followed Galileo over to the Leaning Tower of Pisa where, at the bottom, Tony had pulled the cover off a long, low wooden ramp. At first I was confused. It sure didn't look to me like any fancy science experiment. It looked more like a lane from a bowling alley. One end was *propped up by a large wooden box about the size of a bathtub, giving the thing a low, gentle slope. It all seemed pretty simple. But, as Galileo was about to explain, this simple experiment was about to drive a stake through the heart of two thousand years of bad physics. Or at least that was the plan ...*

Tony snapped to attention as Galileo approached. "The ramp remains in perfect condition, Master."

Galileo shook his head. "For the ten-thousandth time, Tony, just call me Galileo."

Tony bowed low. "Yes, Master."

Galileo sighed and turned toward us. "Anyway, Super Crew, behold my one and only acceleration ramp."

"Cool," Keisha said, trying to pull Bruno back. He was leaning over the wood and sniffing it. "Um, what's the ramp supposed to prove?"

Galileo ignored Bruno's curiosity and beamed proudly. "That objects falling to earth will increase their speed at the exact same rate, regardless of their weight."

I shrugged my shoulders. "Gee, Galileo, you need to prove that? It's just gravity doing its thing."

The great scientist look puzzled. "Eh . . . gravity?"

Keisha leaned down and whispered in my ear. "Max, give him a break. Gravity won't be understood until Isaac Newton comes along."

"Oh," I said.

"Sorry, Galileo," Curtis said. "Just tell us how it works."

"Well, as you can see," the great scientist began, "the ramp is held up at a low angle by that wooden box at the end."

Bruno walked up to the box, spit on his hands, and rubbed them all over the wood.

Galileo looked at us in confusion.

"Um . . . it's for luck," I said, not having the slightest idea as to what Bruno was doing.

"Oh," Galileo replied.

Megan quickly changed the subject. "Wow, this ramp's as smooth as glass."

Galileo shook his head. "Oh yes. I don't want the cannonballs to hit any imperfections as they roll down the slope."

"Cannonballs?" Curtis asked.

"Yes," Galileo replied with a smile. "By rolling cannonballs of different weights down this ramp, I can very simply demonstrate my theory."

"But I don't understand," I said. "Why use the ramp at all? You could just drop the cannonballs from the Leaning Tower or something."

Galileo shook his head. "No, Maximilian. Then the balls would fall much too fast. The ramp slows things down so we can more easily observe them."

"Makes sense," I said. "But how does rolling cannonballs down a ramp help you learn anything?"

Galileo explained. "Simple. By showing that objects with very different weights will always fall side by side, I can prove that Nature has regular laws!"

Megan was unimpressed. "So? What's the big deal about that?"

Galileo explained as best he could. "Regular laws are what the New Science is all about, Super Crew! Just think, if we can learn these laws by carefully observing our experiments, then we can someday hope to understand both ourselves and the great Cosmos around us!"

Wow. I guess that answered her. Megan nodded as Tony clapped and Bruno grunted. At least until Galileo's smile disappeared and his brows knitted together. "But alas, all is not well."

"What's wrong?" Keisha asked.

"My acceleration ramp," he answered with a depressed shrug. "Back in my lab, it gave me the same results each and every time. The heavy cannonball and the light cannonball always rolled past the finish line together."

"And out here on the lawn . . . ?" Keisha continued.

"The heavy one rolls to the finish line first," he said with a sigh. "I don't understand it. If there's nothing wrong with the equipment or the way I'm doing the experiment, then I'll be forced to admit that the New Science is a big, fat flop."

"I don't understand, Galileo," I admitted.

"Think about it, Max," Curtis answered first. "If the same experiment gets different results just because you do it somewhere else, that means there aren't regular laws you can count on."

"Exactly," Keisha nodded. "And those regular laws are what we need to make all our stuff work."

"What stuff?" I asked, still not quite there. Keisha reeled me off a list.

"Oh, airplanes, TVs, stereos, robots, computers, elevators, cars, microwaves."

"Okay, okay," I said. "I get it." I looked up at Galileo. "We'll stay here as long as it takes to get the New Science rolling."

He still looked worried, though. "Thank you, Super Crew. But unfortunately there's a time limit."

"How long do we have?" Curtis asked.

"Until mid-day today. That's when the Prince himself will come to see the New Science in action. If my acceleration ramp fails to prove what I have said it will, then I shall be the laughing stock of all Europe."

"And the New Science will go down the tubes," Keisha said.

"Which would make the future totally different," Megan added.

We looked at each other wide-eyed. This case was a big one.

"The sun will be up soon, Master," Tony spoke up. "These young people must be off. Soon the soldiers of the Inquisition will be afoot."

"Tony is right, Super Crew," Galileo agreed. "You must hide your conveyance in the hills."

"Maybe," I said. "That depends."

Galileo looked surprised. "On what?"

"On what a conveyance is."

Keisha poked me in the arm. "He means our train, doofus. Where will we meet you again, Galileo?"

"In my lab off the town's main *piazza*. You can't miss it. Just look for my trademark."

"Which is . . . ?" Keisha asked.

"A giant pendulum swinging back and forth in front of my door."

"Cool," Curtis said.

"And what about me, Master?" Tony asked.

"You stay here and guard the ramp," Galileo answered.

The assistant looked upset. "But I want to follow in your magnificent shadow."

Galileo shook his head. "No, no. I need you to guard the ramp. I fear the Inquisition is up to some kind of dirty trick."

"Can I applaud you as you walk away?"

Galileo looked embarrassed. "Please don't."

Tony pouted. "Yes, Master."

Galileo slapped his own forehead. "And don't call me . . . Oh, never mind." He looked over at us. "Super Crew, we will meet again soon, eh?"

"You bet, Galileo," Keisha assured him. "Just let us get our train hidden."

"Excellent," he replied. "But be on the lookout for the Inquisition's spies. They're everywhere!"

"Check," Keisha called out as I grabbed Bruno's wrist and we all jogged back to the KC Express.

CHAPTER SIX

Going for Baroque

In order not to attract the attention of the Inquisition, we took Galileo's advice and hid the KC Express in the woods of some nearby hills. Since our train used to be a top-secret military vehicle, we still had a bunch of camouflage netting stored away. When we were done covering everything up, it looked pretty good. At least from a distance.

Anyway, now all we had to do was camouflage ourselves to fit in with the locals. For that there was only one place to go: The Costume Car. Basically, the place is a giant walk-in closet stuffed with masks, wigs, and all sorts of clothes and disguises. Since most of the time we don't go undercover for our cases, it had been a while since any of us had been inside.

Keisha stepped in first, followed by me, Curtis, Megan, and Bruno ...

"Ugh," Keisha said, wiping her hands over her face. "I just stepped through a spider's web."

"A spider?" Curtis's eyes got wide. He didn't like spiders.

"Relax, Can-Do Boy," Megan said. "Bruno's got the problem under control. Look."

The Neanderthal had picked up the spider and was sniffing at it.

Keisha wrinkled her nose. "He's not going to eat that, is he?"

Bruno popped it in his mouth and chewed.

"Yep," I said.

Keisha changed the subject before we all got too grossed out. "Come on, Crew. We've used up thirty minutes just hiding the train. Let's grab some costumes and head out fast."

"What should we wear?" Megan asked.

"I'm not sure," Keisha said. "Let's see if we can get ALEC on the intercom and ask for advice."

"Good idea," I agreed. "The more we blend in the better."

We all looked around the Costume Car for the intercom. Normally, the little wall speaker that hooks into ALEC isn't hard to find. In here it was a different story. Hundreds of costumes lined each side of the car from one end to the other. Along the floor there were boxes and boxes full of shoes and boots and other knickknacks. And, hanging overhead on hooks, were wigs, hats, and fake beards and moustaches.

"Hey, here it is," Megan said, finding ALEC's intercom right behind a shiny suit of armor. She pushed the button. "ALEC? You there?"

"Heelllooo, Crew," the familiar voice called out. "My sensors inform me you've just entered the Costume Car. Planning on attending a masquerade party?"

"More like a Pisa party," Keisha said, giggling at her own pun.

"We need to blend in with the locals as best we can," I said. "Any advice?"

"Ahh, I see," our supercomputer said. "You need to dress for a period historians sometimes refer to as the 'Baroque.' It was an age known for its very fancy tastes in art, architecture, and fashion."

I thought of Galileo's puffy pillow hat, long, flowing cape, and big lace collar. It sure was a lot different than our jeans, T-shirts, and high-tops.

"Yeah, I guess we gotta find some stuff like Galileo wears," I said, opening one of the boxes and rummaging around.

"Hey, how's this?" Curtis called out.

We turned around. He had slipped into a shiny red robe with fancy green dragons sewed on it. He put on the little black hat that went with it and taped a thin black beard under his chin. He looked just like a Chinese noble. "Confucius says," he said with a grin, "man who eat crackers in bed sleep crummy."

"That's pretty good, Curtis," Keisha giggled. "But check *this* out."

She had put on a costume that made her look like Cleopatra from ancient Egypt. The headdress had two golden horns with a disk in the middle that stood for the sun.

"Cool, Keisha," Megan said, slipping into a rhinestone jacket and matching boots and cowboy hat. "But can you *walk* like an Egyptian?"

Keisha could. She put one hand up and out and the other hand back and down, and then shuffled across the floor like she was on a tightrope. Curtis and Megan laughed as they watched her go all the way to the end of the car. It gave me a chance to slip into my costume. "Tah dah!" I said when I was ready. The Crew turned and looked.

"Max!" Megan said, sounding impressed. "You look just like Napoleon Bonaparte!"

"Yeah," Curtis added. "Only taller."

To tell the truth, I felt tall. The General's uniform even came with the big fancy hat and a plastic sword. I stuck one hand under my coat and tried to look intimidating. "From now on, everyone will take their orders from me!"

Keisha tapped me on the shoulder. "Easy, Max. Don't let the threads go to your head."

"Um, Crew," ALEC's voice came over the intercom. "If I might make a suggestion . . ."

"What's up, ALEC?" Megan said, looking for a costume of her own.

"According to my inventory files, there are precisely three outfits which match the ones worn in Galileo's day. Check out coat hangers 51 through 53."

"Hey, yeah," Keisha said, taking a look at the ones ALEC meant. "This stuff should blend in perfectly."

She, Curtis, and Megan hurriedly slipped the costumes over their clothes. It was amazing, with their long flowing capes and high ruffled collars, they looked like people from four hundred years ago.

"Cool, Crew," I said. "But what about me? Don't I get a better costume?"

Keisha looked at me and shrugged. "Sorry, Max. There were only three of these."

"And besides," Curtis added. "The Napoleon costume is the only one small enough to fit you."

He was right, of course. Still, I didn't like hearing it.

Megan looked down at her feet. "Should we find some different shoes or stick with our high-tops?"

"I'm sticking with sneakers," Curtis said. "We may have to come back to the train in a big hurry."

"That's a good point," Keisha agreed. "Let's just hope that no one notices."

We all nodded as Keisha continued. "Well, Crew, are you ready to . . . hey, wait a minute. Where's Bruno?"

The big caveman was nowhere to be seen.

"Bruno?" Megan called out.

There was some rustling down at the far end of the car.

"Bruno?" Megan called out again. "Is that you?"

It was. He stepped out from the hanging rack of clothes. Only this time he'd changed. We all laughed so hard tears came out of our eyes. I'll never figure out how he got it over his elk antlers, but Bruno had slipped into a full-length dress.

"Beautiful," Megan said through her gasps for air. "Now all we gotta do is find him a pair of size sixteen heels."

Bruno laughed when he saw us laughing. The Costume Car wasn't equipped with a video camera and the whole thing made ALEC feel left out. "What's going on, Crew?" he kept asking.

"You missed it, ALEC," Keisha said, wiping away a few tears. "Something funny just 'Baroque' us all up."

She would be laughing at her own pun for at least ten minutes.

CHAPTER SEVEN

Witches and Warlocks

Before we could go help Galileo, we had to figure out one big hairy problem—where to put Bruno while we were gone. If we left the caveman all alone, he could get lost or hurt or something worse. In the end, we did the best we could and set him up in the Bowling Alley Car with a huge bag of popcorn and a case of cold soda. As for ourselves, we went back to the Lab Car so Curtis could load up his gadget pack. That's basically his high-tech security blanket. Whenever we set off on a case, Curtis likes to bring his backpack full of inventions. I don't have a problem with it. Hey, I'd carry a pastry pack if I could get away with it. When

Curtis was all set, we hit the dusty trail to Pisa. We hadn't gone more than ten steps before the train doors shwooshed back open and a familiar howl rose up behind us. Bruno had figured out how to leave the train all by himself...

"Oh no. How'd he learn to do that?" Curtis asked.

"He must be evolving!" I said, impressed. "Good boy, Bruno!"

Keisha rolled her eyes. "Get real, Max. He must have seen us do it."

Bruno trotted toward us like a loyal dog.

"Now I've seen everything," Megan said. "A jogging caveman in bowling shoes and a dress."

"Hey, Max," Keisha said. "I have an idea. Break out the candy bars."

I tried to act ignorant. "Um . . . what do you mean?"

"She means the candy bars you always carry around in your pockets," Megan said. "We all know you have them. Now hand 'em over, Choco Boy."

What could I do? The Crew was on to me. I shrugged and forked over a couple of my Choco-Locos. Megan unwrapped them, stepped toward Bruno, and waved them under his nose. "Want some tooth-decaying, gooey goodness, big boy?"

Bruno sniffed at the chocolate and started to slobber. "*Baka-baka!*" he grunted with a nod.

"I think that means yes, Megan," Curtis commented.

But Megan was already leading Bruno back to the train like a puppy. She got to the Bowling Car, opened the door, threw the candy bars inside, and closed it as soon as he hopped in.

"Now run!" she called out, already heading back toward us in a sprint.

It was hard to run with the bulky costumes on, but we did the best we could. When we were sure Bruno hadn't followed us, we slowed down to a walk and caught our breath.

"Now just remember, everybody," Keisha said, getting her wind back first. "We're going to be fish out of water when we get to Pisa, so let's make sure we don't do anything to get ourselves in trouble."

"Uh oh," I huffed. "It looks like trouble just found us!"

The Crew looked down the trail to see what I was talking about. Four soldiers were approaching on horseback.

"You there!" the one I took to be the officer barked out. "We've had reports of a strange conveyance in this neck of the woods. Have you seen anything unusual?"

We shook our heads as we all answered at once.

"Nope."

"Nothing strange."

"Same old, same old."

"All systems normal."

The officer squinted at us. He was a big guy with red hair who looked just like the kid who used to push me off the swing at recess. The total bully type. The kind of guy who's been sneering so long a smile would crack his face in half. "Say . . . just who *are* you strangers anyway?"

We hadn't prepared ourselves for the question and each of us blurted out a different answer.

"We're tourists."

"We're lost."

"We're with the circus."

"We're real estate agents."

The soldiers drew their swords. I don't think they believed us.

The officer curled his lip. "We've obviously found us some witches and warlocks, men." The soldiers grunted in agreement. "Let's take them to the Inquisition's dungeon and collect our reward!"

The soldiers hopped off their horses and made their way toward us. Without question, It was time for desperate action! Megan was the first to step up to the plate. "All right! So you've figured us out. We *are* witches and warlocks! But you'd better leave us alone because we have magical powers!"

The three soldiers stepped back in fright but the officer sneered even more. "Hah, you young spell-casters don't scare me! You're witches all right, but everybody knows you won't be truly powerful until you're old and green and ugly! Take them away, boys!"

The soldiers stepped forward again, but stopped when Curtis pulled the Boom-Bot from his gadget pack. "You want proof of our powers?" he shouted, his voice high-pitched and nervous. "Well, just listen to this!"

He placed the Boom-Bot on the ground and punched a button on the remote control. The air was filled with the whines and whistles of radio static. The soldiers raised their eyebrows, but they didn't seem too afraid.

"So," the officer hissed. "You young min-ions of darkness have an automaton that squeaks. Is *that* supposed to stop us?"

The soldiers moved toward us again. Curtis, his hands shaking so much he could barely hold the remote control, turned the dial from one end to the other. "What's the deal? Aren't there any stations around here?"

Keisha looked at him like he had lost his mind, which, for the moment, he sort of had. "Get a grip, Curtis! Radio won't be invented for another three hundred years. Switch it to the CD!"

"Oh yeah," Curtis replied just in time. The soldiers were about to pounce on us when the Boom-Bot hit them with a wall of sound. *Aaahhh!! Say you want a Rev - o - lu - tion! Well, you know, we all want to change the world!*

That one did it. The soldiers, their eyes wide in terror, quickly jumped back on their horses. Even the bully officer looked afraid. "You've . . . you've locked men in that little box!"

"Yes, I have," Megan said, wiggling her fingers like she might cast another spell at any moment. "Only I turned them into a bunch of Beatles first!"

"Away, men!" the officer shouted. "We must report these young witches to the Grand Inquisitor!"

He was talking to himself, though. His soldiers were already off and going. The officer turned his horse around and galloped away too. We just stood there and watched him go in a cloud of dust. After a while, our knees stopped shaking and our heartbeats returned to normal. Keisha spoke up first.

"Well, Crew. We've scared 'em away for now, but I have a feeling that won't be the last we'll see of the Inquisition."

Keisha had no way of knowing just how right she'd be!

CHAPTER EIGHT

Into Town

Talk about being fish out of water. We were four kids from the future tromping around a place where just having a different opinion could get you tossed in a dungeon. Or worse even. That's why, after those soldiers rode off, we agreed on a simple plan: help Galileo and get out fast!

The sky had lightened to a pinkish-orange as we made our way through the city gates of Pisa. We tried to keep our cool on the already crowded streets and act as if we belonged, but nobody was fooled. Even little kids could tell we were strangers. Especially considering the way I was dressed. I felt like I was in one of those old Westerns where the whole town freezes as the tough guys come riding in. Only

I didn't feel so tough. Almost every guy we saw had a mean-looking knife or sword. Some of the soldiers even had armor and humongous lances. All we had was Curtis's Boom-Bot and the little plastic sword that went with my Napoleon costume. Still, it was too late to turn back now. We pasted smiles on our faces and marched deeper into town with every muddy step...

"Uh oh," Megan said, "I don't think we're blending in very well."

"It must be our high-tops," Keisha commented.

Curtis wiped some sweat off his forehead with his sleeve. "Uh . . . Max?"

"Yeah?"

"The next time someone calls from the past, just tell them we haven't been born yet, okay?"

"It's not my fault," I said in my own defense. "Megan's the one who hit the Pisa Delivery Switch."

"Hey," she said. "How was I supposed to know it wasn't the hotline to Stuffy's Pizza?"

"Take it easy, Crew." That was Keisha. "I can see the *piazza* up ahead. There're the fountains and market stalls."

I tried to look, but a horse cart went rolling by, blocking my view. It was hauling something that didn't smell too good. Flies swarmed behind like smoke from an exhaust pipe. I waved them off as we passed through. A big mistake on my part.

"You there!" a roar rose up. "Did you just thumb your nose at me, sir?"

I looked up. A young man was staring in my direction. He seemed a little older than Keisha, though not quite as tall. He had a green cloak, brown boots, and a long sword with a golden handle. I turned around to see who he was yelling at.

"What? So the little general turns his back on me, does he?"

"Huh?" I spun around and looked him eye-to-eye. "Are you talking to me?"

81

"Yes, sir. You, sir. The perpetrator of an insult most foul!"

"But . . . but . . ."

He curled his thin mustache. "I demand satisfaction."

"You got me all wrong," I said. "I was only swatting a fly."

"I am Tybalt of the house of Capulet! Not a fly!"

"Gosh. I didn't mean you. I meant a real . . ."

"Draw your steel!"

I blinked. "Draw my steel?" What did that mean? Apparently it meant grab your sword. At least that's what Tybalt did. He had it out as fast as any gunslinger and was slashing fancy patterns in the air.

"I said draw your steel!" he screamed again.

"But . . ."

"Villain!" He sloshed through the mud toward me.

What could I do? I was so scared I pulled my own sword out on pure reflex. Keisha was the first to bring me to my senses.

"Max! What are you doing? That's plastic!"

Tybalt made a quick swipe with his weapon and cut my 'blade' off at the handle. It landed upright in the mud and jiggled back and forth.

"Uh oh," I said, looking at my friends. "Tell my sister she can have my stereo."

But fortunately that wouldn't be necessary. Not with the Crew around to step in and save me in the nick of time. Curtis yanked the Boom-Bot from his gadget pack as Megan clenched her fists and shouted at my attacker. "You leave him alone, you big bully! Or should I use some of my hocus-pocus powers and turn you into a bug?"

Tybalt stopped and looked at Megan a little uncertainly. She didn't miss a beat. She narrowed her eyes and wiggled her fingers like she was about to cast a spell.

"Are . . . are you a witch?" he asked, suddenly not sounding so brave.

"Yeah," Megan said. "But don't take my word for it. Just listen to what these Beatles have to say. Hit it, Curtis."

He did. The Boom-Bot blared out loud and clear.

We all live in a yellow submarine, a yellow submarine, a yellow submarine. We all live . . .

The rest of the song was drowned out by the screams. Quick as a flash, we had cleared the entire block. It gave me a chance to see the whole *piazza*. "Hey," I said. "There's the building with the swinging pendulum!"

"Galileo's lab," Keisha said. "Let's get inside quick."

"Yeah," Curtis agreed. "I don't think we're making a whole lot of new friends out here."

We rushed down the street and into the town's main square, the grand *piazza*. This time, with everybody shouting at each other at the market stalls or drawing water from the fountains, no one even noticed us. Not that we gave them long to look. We dodged the swinging pendulum at Galileo's front door and darted inside.

"Wow!" Megan said, catching her breath. "Between cavemen and sword duels, this case has gotten downright dangerous."

"Tell me about it," I said, still shaking from my sword fight.

"Hey, I have an idea," Curtis piped up. "Let's go home."

Keisha gave him an annoyed look. "We can't do that yet, Curtis. We're stuck here until Max wakes up."

"Yeah," I said. "And besides, Galileo's counting on us."

"Just a thought," he replied.

Keisha softened up. "Look, I'm nervous, too. But the worst part's over. From here on out, I predict smooth sailing."

A sudden scream came from upstairs. It sounded like Galileo.

"You were saying?" Megan said.

But Keisha had already bolted up the steps to see what was wrong. We all shrugged and followed.

"Careful, Keisha," Curtis said as we got to the door at the top of the stairs. "It could be some kind of trap."

Keisha slowly twisted the handle and opened the door. We all pressed our faces to the crack, trying to see inside.

"Hey, he's alone," Megan whispered.

She was right. Galileo stood all by himself at the window, looking up at the sky with a telescope.

"Aaaaha!!!!!" he yelled again.

"Are . . . are you okay, Galileo?" Keisha asked.

He wheeled around with a huge smile on his face. "Oh, Super Crew! Wonderful news!"

"What's up?" I asked.

He looked so excited he was ready to burst. "The Moon has craters!"

We glanced at each other and grinned. All of us had known that since we were little kids.

"Oh really?" Keisha said. "Craters, huh?" She was trying to be nice.

Galileo nodded in excitement. "I've seen them for the first time through my new telescope. Here."

He handed it to me. It was a long brass tube with a couple of glass lenses stuck inside.

"Neat telescope," Keisha said.

"Thanks," Galileo replied. "I built it myself."

"Cool," Curtis said, highly impressed.

"Take a look, Maximilian," Galileo encouraged. "Before the Moon is lost to the day's glare."

I pointed the telescope up at the sky.

"Do you see the Moon?" he asked.

"Uh huh."

"And the craters?" he continued.

"Yep. Like Swiss cheese."

If the high five had been invented, Galileo would've given us one. I've never seen anyone so happy.

"Those craters are more points for the New Science!" he shouted.

"What do you mean?" Keisha asked.

Galileo explained. "Since the time of the ancient Greeks, it's been assumed that everything beyond the Earth is perfect and without flaws of any kind."

"So if the moon has more potholes than Kinetic City Avenue . . ." Curtis thought aloud.

"It's yet more evidence that we have to rethink all that we thought was true!" Galileo finished.

Wow. I was beginning to understand why Galileo was so important. He wasn't just figuring out stuff first, he was kicking off a whole new way of thinking. Pretty cool, huh? But his face soon grew serious again.

"But alas, Super Crew, there is no more time for talk. The morning is upon us. Quickly, help me carry these to the ramp." He pointed to the corner. There lay two shiny cannonballs.

I walked over and tried to pick one up. "Upf," I grunted. "What is this thing made of, lead?"

Galileo nodded. "Actually, yes. Try the other one. It's made of iron and is much lighter."

"But they're the same size," I said, nearly dropping the lead one on my toe.

"Lead is denser than iron," Galileo explained. "So even though the cannonballs have the same volume, the lead one is still heavier."

"Oh," I said, still a little vague. Galileo gave me a real-world example that I could sink my teeth into.

"What weighs more, Maximilian, a cup of melted butter or a cup of whipped cream?"

My Kitchen Car experience made that one easy. "The butter," I answered.

"Exactly," Galileo confirmed. "Even though they both occupy the same amount of space, the butter is denser and therefore heavier. Just like the lead and iron cannonballs."

"Neat," I said, picking up the iron one. It was a lot lighter. I stuffed it under my vest.

Megan folded her arms. "Just what are you doing, Lumpy Boy?"

I scowled like a little dictator and tried my best to look intimidating.

"I am not Lumpy Boy!"

"Oh yeah?" Megan said. "Who are you then?"

"I'm Napoleon *Bowlin'-heart!*"

Personally, I thought it was the best pun I had ever made. Still, only Keisha laughed.

CHAPTER NINE

Down on Gravity

Galileo led us out of Pisa using back streets all the way. Once we were past the city gates, we made a beeline for the acceleration ramp where Tony was still standing guard. Around him was a group of six or seven young men, all dressed in monks' robes. They took off in the opposite direction when they saw us coming ...

"Who were your friends, Tony?" Galileo asked, setting his cannonball down with a thud behind the starting gate.

The teaching assistant bowed low. "Fellow students, Master. We were having a debate as to whether the Sun goes around the Earth, or the Earth goes around the Sun."

I plopped my own cannonball down. It was a lot lighter than Galileo's. Still, my arms felt a couple of inches longer.

"A debate, eh?" Galileo repeated. "So what were your conclusions?"

"I, of course, said the Earth orbits the Sun," Tony responded. "Just like you taught me."

Galileo nodded. "Excellent. And what was their reply?"

"They said that only a fool would claim the Earth moved. If it spun around so fast, we would never be able to stand on it."

Curtis laughed. "I made the same mistake on a test last year, Tony."

Galileo's assistant looked at Curtis. "What do you mean?"

Curtis explained. "We're able to stand on the Earth because we're *stuck* to it. Gravity holds us down and we spin with it. That way it only *looks* like the Earth isn't moving."

Tony scratched the inside of his ear with a finger. I don't think he got it. Curtis didn't have time to explain more, though. Galileo was clapping his hands. "Come, Super Crew, we will have to convince them of their error some other day. As for now, keep your eyes open as we release the cannonballs."

"What exactly do you need us to watch for?" I asked.

"Tell me whether or not they finish in a tie."

"You were getting ties in your lab, right, Galileo?" Keisha said.

The great scientist nodded. "Yes. Each and every time. Out here though, the lead one is going faster. Unless we can find something wrong with the experiment itself, my theory will soon flop in front of the Prince."

"Why's that again?" I asked.

Galileo explained it once more. "You see, Maximilian, in order for the New Science to work, the same experiment must produce the exact same results. Otherwise, it would be impossible to make accurate predictions or uncover natural laws."

"Oh," I said. "That makes sense."

"And the Prince is expecting the cannon-balls to finish neck and neck, huh?" Curtis said.

Galileo nodded. "That's what I promised him. Now, is everyone ready?"

"Let 'em roll, Galileo," I said, leaning my head over the end of the ramp.

Megan plopped down in the grass across from me. "Yep. All set. Bowl us over, Gravity Boy."

"Okay," Galileo cried. "On three. *Uno . . . due . . . tre!*"

Galileo's teaching assistant opened the starting gate. The lead cannonball took off first and stayed out in front all the way down. It rolled past my nose and went into the grass for an easy win.

Keisha, Curtis, and Megan all stared in shock. From their high school science courses, they knew that wasn't the result the textbooks said would happen. Curtis whistled long and low. "Wow. Something weird is definitely going on."

Megan nodded. "Yeah, but what? The

whole thing's so simple. What could possibly be wrong?"

"Maybe this force you call gravity just doesn't work here out on the lawn," Galileo suggested.

Keisha shook her head. "I don't think so, Galileo. Speaking as a representative of the future, I can promise you gravity is about as universal as it gets."

"Drats!" Galileo yelled, losing his cool. He kicked the wooden box that propped up the ramp. "Ouch!" He hopped up and down holding his toe.

"Hey," Curtis said, getting an idea from Galileo's injury. "Maybe Galileo could show that every action has an equal and opposite reaction instead."

Keisha shook her head. "Nah. That's another Isaac Newton thing."

We were so busy watching Galileo jump up and down that we didn't see the man on the horse until he was right behind us. The rider was dressed much like Galileo, complete with the puffy hat. I don't think anybody else saw it, but I noticed that Tony bowed extra low to him. I wondered why.

"Greetings, Galileo!" the rider called out.

An annoyed look flashed across Galileo's face. Still, he was polite enough. "*Ciao*, Aristortelini."

I blinked. "Aristortelini? Isn't your name a lot like . . ."

The rider nodded as he correctly guessed my question. "Yes it is. I am named after the great philosopher Aristotle as well as my mamma's favorite pasta. Do you have a problem with that?"

I shook my head. "No. No. Not at all." I figured my sleeping brain was having a hard time coming up with good names for all these dream characters.

Aristortelini refocused his attention on Galileo. "So, your big day has arrived. Word has it the Prince is most interested to see if your New Science is all it's cracked up to be."

"Is that all you've come to say?" Galileo asked. I could tell the two didn't much like each other.

"Not at all, dear friend," Aristortelini said smoothly. "I've come to wish you good luck."

Galileo nodded. "Thank you."

"Good luck in finding a job after your New Science flops!" he laughed.

"It won't flop," I shouted. "There's still time to figure out what's wrong!" Whoops. Sometimes I say too much.

Aristortelini smiled in a way that made him look like a lizard. "What? Is something wrong?"

Galileo shook his head. "No. Everything is fine."

"So you'll still have the demonstration at noon?"

"Of course," Galileo said. "I have no choice."

Aristortelini smiled his lizard smile again. "Excellent. You know, Galileo, sometimes I pity you. You waste your good mind on useless experiments when everything's been figured out already."

"Hah! That's what you think, Buster," Megan piped up. "Where we come from, there's all kinds of stuff you guys don't know."

"Oh really," Aristortelini said sarcastically. "And where is it you come from?"

"From the fut . . ." Megan stopped herself just in time. I had a feeling that giving that fact away could prove bad for our health.

Aristortelini raised his eyebrows. "From where?"

"Uh . . . from *Defut*," Keisha spoke up quickly. "We come from the tiny fishing village of Defut."

"Never heard of it," he said.

"It's in France," Keisha said.

"Ah, I see," Aristortelini replied, nodding at me. "I suppose that explains why the little one is dressed so . . . extravagantly."

I made a mental note to stock the Costume Car with more stuff in my size.

"Oh, and by the way, Galileo," Aristortelini grinned. "I almost forgot. The Inquisition has arrested a warlock. You're invited if you want to watch the interrogation. It might do you good to see what you're in for if you don't cease this ridiculous experimentation."

"What are you talking about, Aristortelini?" Galileo snorted in disgust. "There's no such thing as a real warlock. Only the unlucky souls mistaken for them."

Aristortelini shook his head. "That's what you think, Galileo. But this one is the real deal. The brute was found roaming the woods in elk antlers and a dress. He also had very strange shoes and a necklace of pungent charms."

Our eyes shot open wide. Bruno!

"The warlock possesses incredible strength," Aristortelini continued. "It took ten soldiers to bring him in. Their broken bones will take weeks to heal."

"Is . . . is the warlock okay?" I asked.

Aristortelini looked down his nose at me. "He's fine, French boy. But not for long. The Grand Inquisitor will soon force him to admit to his evil ways."

"Where is he now?" Keisha asked, trying to sound nonchalant.

"Why, I told you already. He's having lunch with the Prince."

Keisha shook her head. "No. I mean the warlock."

Aristortelini sneered. "That brute is where he belongs. Locked in the deepest dungeon of the Inquisition's impenetrable fortress!"

Yikes! We could tell at a glance that each of us was thinking the exact same thing—rescue Bruno and fast!

"Very well, Galileo!" Aristortelini called out, turning his horse back toward town. "I shall return in an hour to watch you fail miserably! Then your professorship will go to me. Hah! Wait . . . double that. Hah-hah!" He spurred his horse and galloped off.

"Who was he?" Curtis asked Galileo.

"A representative of the old school," the great scientist responded. "He believes that Aristotle's physics will never be proved wrong."

"Oh," Keisha said. "But what was that part about your job going to him?"

Galileo nodded. "Alas, it is true. If my demonstration fails to convince the Prince, then Aristortelini will get my professorship."

Megan watched Aristortelini gallop away. "Gee. What a creep," she sneered.

"Yeah," I said. "I wouldn't even trust that guy for bad directions."

But we didn't have a lot of time to hang around and bad-mouth Aristortelini. Keisha was already calling a huddle so we could make our plans.

"Okay, Crew," she said. "We've got one hour to do two things: figure out what's wrong with the acceleration ramp, and rescue Bruno. Since the second job is a lot riskier, I say we do rock, paper, scissors to see who goes. Ready?"

We all nodded.

"Right," Keisha said. "One, two, three."

Curtis and Megan both chose rocks. Keisha and I both chose paper. Paper covers rock. We would help Galileo while they rescued Bruno.

"Hey, wait a minute," Curtis said. "I was going to choose scissors. Really. My fingers just got stuck."

"C'mon, Curtis," I said. "Keisha and I won fair and square. Of course, it doesn't hurt any that it's my dream."

"All right," he said. "I'll go break out Bruno. But the next time *I* have a weird dream, Max, *you're* doing the dangerous stuff!"

CHAPTER TEN

Mission Improbable— Part 1

There was no time to lose. Curtis strapped on his gadget pack extra tight and he and Megan went back through the city walls with a mission to rescue Bruno. Keeping to the back streets all the way, they soon made it to the Inquisition's giant fortress in the center of town.

"Okay," Curtis said, trying not to sound too scared—which he was. "Now what?"

Megan shook her head. "Hold on. I'm working on it."

They were hidden behind some huge rain barrels directly in front of the Inquisition's main gate. Getting in wouldn't be easy. Armed soldiers kept riding in and out.

"Aww, this is hopeless," Curtis said. "We'll never get in there."

"Never say never, Curtis," Megan said, trying to sound brave but just sounding nervous. "Something will come along."

An ox cart rolled by filled with hay. Megan poked Curtis in the shoulder. "See what I said? Here's our chance!"

"Huh?"

But Megan had already jumped from behind the rain barrel and crawled under the loose hay. Curtis couldn't see her, but he could hear her whisper to him from the back of the cart. "Psst! C'mon! It's now or never!"

"Oooh . . ." Curtis groaned as he traded his perfectly safe hiding place for a perfectly dangerous one.

"Ouch!" Megan whispered.

"What?" Curtis whispered back.

"Your gadget pack just poked me in the ear."

"Oh, sorry."

"Ssh," Megan hushed. "They're opening the gates for the cart."

It was true. There was a loud clanking sound as the heavy metal gate was raised for the cart to roll through. Megan and Curtis felt themselves lurch forward and then the gate fall shut with a bang.

"We're in!" Megan whispered.

"Yeah. But how do we get out?"

"Details, Curtis. We'll worry about that after we find Bruno."

The cart came to a stop and, after waiting a full five minutes, Megan cautiously poked her head through the hay. "Hey, now's our chance. No one's around."

Curtis poked his head out and looked around. Bits of hay dangled from his hair. "Where are we?"

Megan shrugged. "Some kind of inner courtyard. I think this is where they do the wash."

"How can you tell?"

"Look behind you."

Curtis turned his head. Sure enough, a thick clothesline was stretched from one wall to the other. Hanging down from it were a number of big brown robes with hoods. One even had a scarlet 'T' sewn on it. Just like the kind Galileo's assistant Tony wore.

"Are you thinking what I'm thinking, Megan?"

"That Italian fashion's come a long, long way?"

"No, that the Inquisition has supplied us with some better disguises," he said.

"You ready?" Megan whispered. "We've got to do this without anyone seeing us."

Curtis nodded. Megan took one last look around to make sure nobody was watching.

"Now!" she cried.

Curtis and Megan leapt from their hiding place and ran to the clothesline, grabbing three of the big brown robes, two for themselves and one for Bruno after they found him.

"Pull the hood over your head, Curtis," Megan said. "That way nobody will know who we are."

"Check."

They quickly pulled the robes over themselves. Luckily, the things were long enough to cover their shoes. Just in time, too. A familiar voice filled the courtyard.

"There you are!" It was Aristortelini! "I've been looking all over for you, Tony."

Oh no! Curtis had accidentally put on the robe with the scarlet 'T'! He bent down low to hide his face as Aristortelini walked up close.

"It will be high noon in less than an hour. Have you placed the extra lodestones under the ramp as I instructed? I don't want those two cannonballs to be even close."

Curtis didn't dare say a word. Not only would Aristortelini realize he wasn't Tony, he had no idea what a lodestone even was. Megan jumped in to make the save.

"Yes, yes, Aristortelini. All the lodestones are in place. I helped Tony myself."

The man smiled like a lizard with a bug in its mouth. "Excellent. With those lodestones under the ramp, Galileo's great experiment will fail for sure!"

"Yes. Yes," Megan nodded hard, getting the hood to fall even further over her face. "The New Science doesn't stand a chance."

Aristortelini's eyebrows raised suspiciously. "Say . . . isn't your voice a little high to be a monk?"

"Um . . . um . . ." Megan stuttered. "I'm in the choir."

"Oh." Aristortelini said. "Oh, of course."

He changed the subject. "Anyway, you two should hurry up and stake out your seats in the main courtyard. The Grand Inquisitor is about to get some giant brute to admit he's a warlock. It should be quite a show."

Curtis's and Megan's eyes grew wide. He was talking about Bruno!

"Um, where is Brun . . . er, the brute now?" Megan asked.

"Why, in cell 101 of the deepest dungeon,

of course," Aristortelini replied. "The place we throw all the witches. Apparently there are four more at large. Young ones. Soldiers have seen them roaming the hills. We'll get them soon."

"Oh, I hope so," Megan said.

Aristortelini looked down at Curtis and patted him on the hump. "You've done a good job, Tony. What do you have to say for yourself?"

Oh no! Trapped again. Curtis bent over and started coughing as loud as he could. Aristortelini looked alarmed.

"But . . . but what is wrong?"

Curtis kept coughing as Megan answered.

"Oh, don't worry. Tony will be all right. It's just a mild touch of the plague."

Aristortelini's eyes grew wide. *"The plague!"*

"Yeah," Megan said. "You wouldn't happen to have an aspirin on you, would you?"

But Aristortelini was already off and running. "Be gone, Tony!" he shouted over his shoulder. "And never come near me again!"

Curtis and Megan both looked up as Aristortelini disappeared full speed down a hallway.

"Good job, Megan," Curtis said, genuinely impressed.

"Thanks. I do my best work under pressure."

"Sounds like Tony's full of baloney, huh?" Curtis said.

"A regular Benedict Arnold Boy," Megan agreed.

"We've gotta warn Galileo."

Megan nodded. "Check. But first let's get down to the dungeon and break out Bruno before the Grand Inquisitor gets his mitts on him!"

Curtis's knees were still shaking from the close call. Megan's idea didn't exactly help them stop. "I was afraid you were going to say that!"

CHAPTER ELEVEN

A Clown Around

Keisha knew from her science class that something was fishy with Galileo's acceleration ramp. Those cannonballs should have rolled down neck and neck. That's just the way gravity works. Obviously something weird was going on. But what? And how?

We decided our best bet was to set up a stakeout. For that there was only one place that would do—the top of the Leaning Tower itself. So, as Megan and Curtis hurried off to save Bruno, Keisha and I headed up the crooked staircase for an eagle's-eye view of the lawn below. When we were all set up, we used the Can-Do Communicator to run some things by ALEC ...

"You there, ALEC?" I said into the speaker.

"Heeelllooo, Max," his voice crackled out. "Would you like to know how many toothpicks it takes to reach the Moon? I can calculate that. Hold on while I check!"

"No, ALEC," Keisha called out before our computer busied himself with a worthless computation. "We need you to help us with something more important."

"Yeah," I said, nodding my head. "Like Galileo's experiment."

"Oh yes," ALEC replied. "The Galileo problem. How's that going anyway?"

"Horribly," Keisha admitted. "The caveman's been captured and Curtis and Megan have to sneak into a fortress and rescue him."

"Oh my," ALEC beeped.

"And I almost got shish-kebabbed by some nut with a sword," I said.

"Oh my."

"And we got half of Pisa thinking we're witches," Keisha said.

"Oh my."

"And we've only got an hour or so to figure out what's wrong before Galileo's demonstration is a big fat flop," I added.

"Oh my," ALEC beeped again. "Makes me glad that computers don't have dreams."

"I bet," Keisha said. "Now could you help us figure out what's going wrong?"

"Sure," he replied. "Just give me all the info you've got."

I did the best I could to explain exactly what we had seen. When I was done, ALEC beeped a few times before responding. "You really have a juicy mystery here, Crew. The Earth's gravity should pull objects toward it at the same rate, regardless of how much they weigh."

"We know, we know," I said.

"The only thing I can guess is that friction might be your culprit."

"What do you mean?" I asked.

"Those cannonballs are rubbing against the air and against the ramp as they roll. That's friction."

"But ALEC," I said, glancing at the ramp far below. "It's as smooth as glass."

"I see," ALEC said. "But what about the cannonballs? Did they both look nice and round?"

"They looked just fine," Keisha replied.

"Well then I'm stumped," ALEC beeped. "There's still friction going on, of course—you never eliminate it completely unless you're out in space—but the smoothness of the ramp and cannonballs means friction alone shouldn't have the effect you're describing."

"That's what I figured, ALEC," Keisha said. "So, any other info you can give us?"

"Absolutely! Did you know the density of lead is greater than the density of iron?" ALEC asked.

"Yeah," I nodded. "That's what Galileo said."

"Oh," ALEC said, sounding a little jealous that Galileo had beat him to the punch. "Would you like to know some more differences between iron and lead?"

Keisha and I looked at each other and shrugged. "Sure, why not?" she said. "No one's even near the ramp and we've got some time to kill."

Our computer beeped happily and, as usual, gave us more than we really wanted. "Well, to begin, lead has 82 protons stuffed inside its central nucleus while iron has only 26. Also, lead melts at 327.5 degrees Centigrade while iron stays solid until a toasty 2,750."

I quickly changed my mind about wanting to hear all this. "ALEC," I said.

"Iron is also magnetic while lead isn't."

"ALEC," I said even louder.

Our computer beeped. "Yes?"

"That's enough."

He let out a slow, disappointed beep. He can be really sensitive if he thinks we don't need him. Keisha popped another question to perk him back up. "So, um . . . what'll happen if Galileo flops, ALEC?"

"That's impossible to say," our computer answered with some thoughtful beeps. "Galileo's laws of motion really got modern science rolling. If it doesn't happen here and now, then it's possible that the entire history of the world could change."

My eyes grew wide. "Whoa! That big? This case is huge!"

A squeaky voice interrupted us from behind. "Could you two keep it down? I'm trying to sleep."

Keisha and I whipped around. No one was there. Except for a pile of old newspapers, the top of the Leaning Tower was completely empty.

"Freaky," I whispered.

"I still hear you," the high-pitched voice sang out.

"Who . . . who said that?" Keisha demanded.

The newspapers rustled and a face half-coated with gray whiskers poked out. "Me," the man said. "Now that I'm awake that is." He stood up slowly and stretched in the bright morning sun.

"Hey, who's there, Crew?" ALEC's voice crackled over the communicator.

I couldn't give him an answer. Not because I was afraid, I was just too amazed for words. The man was the strangest-looking guy I had ever seen. For starters he was tiny. Much shorter than me even. His clothes were also weird: lime green tights, a bright red jacket, and a goofy, multicolored hat that looked like a stuffed octopus glued to his head. Little bells on the tips of the arms jingled as he brushed his teeth with his finger. He caught me staring at him out of the corner of his eye.

"Yah need somethin', Napoleon?"

"Who *are* you?" I asked.

He finished brushing his teeth before answering. It didn't take long. There weren't many left. "I'm Thadius B. Finkleholler, a Time Tramp just like yourselves."

I shook my head. "We're not Time Tramps . . . at least I don't think so."

The little man scoffed and nodded toward the communicator I was holding. "Sure, General. Then where'd you get the fancy walkie-talkie? Or those space-age running shoes?"

"Okay, you're right, Mr. Finkleholler," Keisha admitted. "We *do* come from the future. But we're not Time Tramps. Whatever one of those is anyway."

The man's miniature eyebrows furrowed in confusion. "But . . . but if you're not Time Tramps, how could you possibly be . . . " His puzzled expression left as quickly as it had come. "Wait a minute! Am I in someone's dream here?"

Keisha pointed at me. "Yeah. We're in his."

"Ah hah," he said, snapping his little fingers. "So our currents got crossed, did they? Well, it's rare, but I've heard of it happening."

"What are you talking about?" I asked.

"Listen, Napoleon, I couldn't explain it even if I wanted to. Just take my word for it, in a few moments we'll lose the connection and I'll pop out of your head forever. Um, anything you wanna ask before I go? I've been around a bit, you know."

I shrugged and asked him the first thing that came to mind. "Okay. Why are you dressed like a court jester?"

"I'm working my way through history as a clown."

"Oh."

He nodded. "Yeah. No matter where I am, if I can make 'em laugh, I'll get a meal."

He pulled out a weathered pack of cigarettes and looked inside. It appeared to be empty. "Um, I don't suppose you kids smoke, do you?"

I shook my head. "No way."

"Mmm, figures." He wadded up his cigarette pack and stuffed it back in his pocket. "So where are we anyway? I got in before dawn."

"Galileo's Italy," Keisha answered.

His little eyes lit up. "Oh yeah? I've been through here before. Interesting times. Watch out for those Inquisition types, though. They're a walking case of heartburn, I tell yah."

"Hey," Keisha said. "Maybe you can help us with our case. We're trying to figure out what's going wrong with Galileo's big experiment."

"The one where he shows how a swinging pendulum can accurately measure time?"

"No," Keisha said. "The one where he shows how everything falls toward the Earth at the same rate."

"Oh, the acceleration ramp thing," the man said. "Yeah, there's a problem with it. Gets fixed though."

My eyes lit up. "Yeah? How?"

"A group of kids help him figure out what's wrong." The man glanced back down at our running shoes. "Eh, I assume that must be you guys."

"That's us," Keisha confirmed. "But we only have an hour or so. What do we do?"

The man shook his head. "Sorry. Can't tell you that. Against the rules. I can only say you do what you always have done, and the future arrives like it always will."

I whistled softly. "Whoa. Deep."

He shrugged. "Not really. Human history hasn't been around long enough to be truly deep."

"What do you mean?" Keisha asked. "It's thousands of years old."

The man laughed so hard his entire body jiggled, what little there was of it anyway. "Thousands of years, huh?" he giggled. "That's barely enough time for some half-decent tramping."

"It is?" I asked in amazement.

He nodded. "It's like swimming in the baby pool while waiting for the ocean to form. Let human history go from thousands to millions of years. Then we'll talk deep!"

I cocked my head from side to side. The Time Tramp was the strangest character I had ever met. "So you won't tell us what's wrong with the ramp?"

"What? And spoil all your fun?"

"Well, what about a hint?" I guess I can be a stubborn kid at times.

"Sorry." Mr. Finkleholler shook his head so that the little bells jingled.

I broke into my emergency strategy, the one I use on my mom whenever I want to stay up late on a school night. "Oh please, oh please, oh please, oh please!"

Mr. Finkleholler rolled his eyes and raised his tiny hand to stop me. "Okay, okay, already. I'll give you a hint."

"Thank you!" Keisha and I both said at once, leaning in closer to catch what his squeaky voice had to say.

He gave us a funny grin and said only: "You'll iron out the problem."

I shook my head in confusion. "That's it? But you already said that."

"No, I didn't. I only said that it gets fixed. Now I'm saying you'll iron it out."

"But what's the diff . . ." I didn't get a chance to finish my question. The Time Tramp vanished in a sudden puff of smoke. All that was left was a tiny, bluish cloud that slowly wafted away.

Keisha had to tap me on the shoulder to get my attention. "Man, Max, just how bizarre is it inside your head, anyway?"

I defended myself. "What're you talking about? That was Thadius B. Finkleholler, Time Tramp. Our currents got crossed."

Keisha eyed me as though trying to figure out what size straightjacket I'd eventually wear. "Max, we're in your dream, remember?"

She had a point. Time Tramps don't really exist. Still . . . sure seemed real.

"Max, look!" Keisha whispered, pointing down at the ramp.

I turned so fast that Keisha had to grab me by my belt to keep me from losing my balance at the edge. While we were talking to the Time Tramp, Tony and his mysterious buddies had come back to the ramp. I counted six. Each carried a large rock that must have been heavy because I could see them straining.

"What are they doing?" I whispered.

Keisha shook her head. "I don't know."

They put the rocks down. Then, as five of them lifted the heavy ramp, Tony stacked the rocks inside the box, just under the starting gate. We were really high up, but I could see that there were already some rocks in there.

"Now why would they do that?" I asked as they nailed the box shut and placed the ramp back on top of it.

"I don't know," Keisha said. "But it looks awfully suspicious."

The men scurried away.

"C'mon," Keisha said. "Let's go see if Galileo knows about this."

CHAPTER TWELVE

Mission Improbable— Part 2

When Aristortelini spilled the beans about lodestones being planted under the acceleration ramp, Curtis and Megan didn't have a clue what he was talking about. They figured it was important, but it would have to wait until they rescued Bruno. According to Aristortelini, our favorite caveman was being held in a cell on the lowest level of the dungeon. To make matters even worse, the Grand Inquisitor was about to try and force him to admit to being a warlock.

Megan and Curtis had to get Bruno out of there and fast! Safe for the moment in their *monk disguises, they wandered the fortress until they found what they were looking for ...*

"Here they are, Curtis," Megan said. "The stairs to the dungeon."

"Are you sure?" he asked.

"Look at the sign," she pointed.

He looked at the small plaque over the entrance and read it out loud. "Stairway to dungeon. Abandon all hope, all ye who enter here." He gulped. "Yikes. Are we 'ye'?"

Megan shook her head. "Nah. We're from the future. Doesn't apply to us. C'mon."

They took the steps all the way down until they came to a dark, musty hallway.

"Yeech," Megan said, curling her nose. "Doesn't anybody ever mop around here?"

Just then a familiar howl came from the far end of the hall. *"Aaruu!"*

Curtis and Megan looked at each other and spoke at once. "Bruno!"

Megan took a burning torch off its holder on the wall. "Here. Hold this."

Curtis grabbed it and ran it close to the floor. Giant spiders scurried out of the light in every direction. Curtis gulped. "On second thought, I'd just as soon not see anything down here. You take it." He handed the torch back to Megan.

"*Aaruu!*" the caveman's howl came again.

"C'mon!" Megan said. "It came from this way."

They hurried down a side hallway in the direction of the sound.

Sure enough, at the very end they saw a guard standing in front of a locked cell. He was holding a torch of his own and laughing. "Hah hah! You think this is hot? Wait until you feel the heat of the Grand Inquisitor!"

"*Eeooor!*" Bruno howled as the guard taunted him with the flame.

"What do we do now, Megan?" Curtis whispered.

"Follow my lead," she whispered back.

"What are you going to do?"

Megan's face looked freaky in the firelight. "I don't know yet. Just follow my lead, okay?"

Curtis shrugged. "It's worked so far."

Megan took a deep breath, turned around and walked straight up to the guard.

"The Grand Inquisitor says you can go, guard. We'll take over from here."

The guard whipped around, surprised he wasn't alone. "What? The Inquisitor has sent two monks to guard this fearsome warlock?"

"We're not monks," Megan shot back. "We're inquisitors."

"Hah," the guard laughed. "You two pups don't look old enough to be inquisitors."

"Um . . . we're new," Curtis said.

The guard looked at them suspiciously with his one eye and scratched the stubble on his face with the dirtiest fingernails Curtis or Megan had ever seen.

"So, what horrible tortures do you have in mind for this one?" he asked, giving them a test.

"Something fiendish," Megan shot back, her eyes narrowing into tiny slits of blood lust.

"Fiendish, eh?"

"You bet," Curtis said, nodding his head. "Something super-duper fiendish."

"Hmm," the man thought out loud. "You rookies talk a good game, but maybe I should just wait around until the Grand Inquisitor himself shows up."

"Sure," Megan said, sounding like she wanted him to stay. "That'd be great. But then you'd miss out on all that warm gruel they're giving away in the kitchen."

The guard's good eye shot open wide. "What? *Warm* gruel? Are you sure?"

Curtis nodded. "Yep. I just had three big bowls myself."

"And I had two," Megan added quickly. "It's the greatest gruel I've ever gulped."

The man's face looked excited. And hungry. At least judging by the drool that bubbled from the corners of his mouth. It was pretty gross. "Does . . . does this so-called gruel have boiled pigs' tails?"

"That depends," Megan said carefully. "Are boiled pigs' tails good?"

The guard looked so hungry that he almost started to cry. "Boiled pigs' tails are the food of the angels!"

"Then yes," Megan said evenly. "The gruel is loaded with pigs' tails."

"I couldn't even finish all of mine," Curtis added. It wasn't necessary though. The man was already running down the hall. Megan calmly grabbed the keys and opened the gate. Bruno hopped out at once and picked them both up in a massive bear hug.

"Upf," Curtis grunted. "We're glad to see you, too, Bruno. But put us down already."

The caveman seemed to understand and set them both lightly on their feet.

"Great," Megan said. "Now let's go!"

"Not'a so fast," a thick Italian accent behind them said.

Megan and Curtis turned. "Tony!"

"In the flesh," he hissed.

Megan's eyes narrowed. "You've sabotaged Galileo's big experiment."

"Yes, I have," the villain admitted. "Once

Galileo's New Science flops, his professorship will go to my true master, the great Aristortelini!"

"That jerk," Megan sneered. "He isn't fit to teach water safety to goldfish!"

"Enough!" Tony shouted. "You meddlesome kids will never leave this dungeon to tell the tale."

"Oh yeah? How you gonna stop us?" Megan taunted. "Pull a big sword out of thin air?"

Tony reached behind his back and pulled out a big sword. It looked awfully sharp.

"Good job, Megan," Curtis said sarcastically. "Just make him mad, why dont'cha?"

"Silence!" Tony shouted. "And get in that cell. All three of you."

"Okay, okay," Megan said, thinking as fast as she could. "You can hold us here forever, but you can't stop the future from coming. It's still *thumbs up* for Galileo and his New Science!"

"Wrong!" Tony yelled, sticking out his free hand with the thumb turned toward the ground. "It's *thumbs down* for Galileo and for you!"

"Uh huh. And what is it for Aristortelini?" Megan asked quickly.

"A big thumbs up!" he cried, flipping his hand over. Tough luck for him. Big Bruno could not understand what was going on, but he sure knew when he'd been insulted. Quick as a tiger, he jumped forward and knocked the sword out of Tony's hand. The villain screamed and tried to run away, but Bruno grabbed him and held him upside down by an ankle.

"No fair! No fair!" Tony shouted.

"Tell it to the judge, Traitor Boy," Megan said.

"Drop him in here, Bruno," Curtis said, motioning for the caveman to dump Tony in the cell. As soon as he did, Megan shut the door and locked it.

"You'll never get away with this!" Tony spat.

"Oh, yes we will," Curtis said. "You want to know why?"

"Why?"

"Because in the future, Galileo's famous and no one's ever heard of Aristortelini!"

As the villain jumped up and down and yelled all kinds of really nasty words, Megan and Curtis calmly got Bruno into his monk disguise and made their great and daring escape—straight out the front gate of the fortress in plain sight!

CHAPTER THIRTEEN

Back at Galileo's Lab

Meanwhile, back at the ramp, Keisha and I had climbed down from the Leaning Tower to go check out what Tony and his buddies had done to Galileo's experiment. A few minutes earlier, we had watched from above as they loaded a bunch of rocks into the box that held up the ramp. Did Galileo know about this? There was only one way to find out. Keisha and I headed back into town, sticking to the back streets all the way. Once we got to Galileo's, we dodged the swinging pendulum in front of his door and climbed the stairs. We found him leaning out the window, looking through his telescope ...

"Amazing!" he said, not yet realizing we had rushed into the room. "Simply amazing. I don't believe my own eyes!"

"More Moon craters?" I asked.

Galileo wheeled around. Once again he had a huge smile on his face. "No, Maximilian. This time it is your comrades who are so incredible."

"What do you mean?" Keisha asked.

"Here," Galileo said, "take a look." He handed Keisha the telescope and pointed out the window. "Observe those three figures running across the square."

Keisha went to the window and raised the telescope to her eye.

"I watched them march out of the Inquisition's fortress two minutes ago," Galileo continued.

Keisha caught a glimpse of their feet. Two pairs of running shoes and one pair of big, hairy feet. "Curtis and Megan and Bruno!"

"They made it!" I shouted.

"Your friends are very resourceful," Galileo said, highly impressed. "No one's ever escaped from that fortress before."

"We're not called the Super Crew for nothing, Galileo," I said proudly.

He looked at me and smiled. "I believe you, Maximilian." But a worried expression quickly came over him again. "But alas, we've so little time. Have you two discovered anything new?"

I nodded enthusiastically. "You bet. We saw Tony and his buddies fill up the wooden box under the ramp."

Galileo's eyes went wide in surprise. "With what?"

Keisha shook her head. "We're not sure. They looked like some kind of rocks."

"Lodestones, to be exact," Megan shouted from the stairway.

"Lodestones?" Galileo said.

"Lodestones?" Keisha and I repeated.

"Lodestones!" Curtis shouted, stepping into the room in his big brown robe. "Aristortelini and Tony are in cahoots."

We took a quick moment to exchange a round of well-deserved high fives.

"How did you two do it?" Keisha asked Megan.

"I'll explain later," she replied. "Right now we have to worry about those lodestones."

"What exactly is a lodestone?" I asked.

"Aha!" Galileo shouted, finally understanding. "Now I get it! So *that's* how the villains were foiling my experiment! Lodestones are magnets!"

"Ahhh," Megan, Curtis, and Keisha said, getting that old well-I-guess-that-explains-that expression. Only Bruno and I still looked confused. "Um," I said. "Can someone explain it to Bruno, please?"

Keisha helped me out. "Max, remember what ALEC told us on top of the Leaning Tower?"

I thought back. "That he can calculate how many toothpicks it takes to reach the Moon?"

Keisha shook her head. "No, not that. The differences between lead and iron."

"Yeah, I remember," I said. "Lead's denser."

Keisha nodded. "Yeah. And it also isn't magnetic. Iron is."

I remembered that. Still . . . "Yeah. So?"

"Think about it," she said. "If a bunch of magnets are stacked up under the iron cannonball at the starting gate . . ."

That was enough. I had it. "Then the iron cannonball would be slowed down," I said. "And the heavy lead cannonball would roll to the bottom first." The others nodded. Now only Bruno still looked confused.

"Wow," Curtis said. "Talk about a low-down trick."

"Come!" Galileo shouted. "There is no time to lose. We must remove the lodestones at once!"

"I don't think we can in time," Keisha said.

"Eh? What do you mean?" Galileo asked.

"It's almost noon," she answered. "It's time for your presentation to the Prince."

Galileo looked really hurt and worried. "Hurry, Super Crew," he pleaded. "We must think of something! The Prince must not be kept waiting!"

What could we do? There wasn't enough time to remove the lodestones. Besides, even if we did, Aristortelini would know that we were on to him. It was time for a stroke of genius. I thought about the Time Tramp's hint, the one where he said I'd 'iron out' the problem. It didn't seem to help much. Then, as if the classic lightbulb lit up my entire brain . . .

"I've got it!"

"Got what, Max?" Megan asked skeptically.

"The solution!"

"Oh yeah?" she said, even more skeptical.

"Yeah," I said. "I just figured out the Time Tramp's hint!"

"What are you talking about?" Megan asked.

"Keisha will explain," I said excitedly. "But for now go to the ramp and keep the Prince busy. I'll be there soon. C'mon, Bruno!" I added, waving for the caveman to follow me. "I'm gonna need your muscle power."

CHAPTER FOURTEEN

Bowling for Science

With literally minutes to go, Bruno and I ran back to the KC Express to pick up what I needed for my big idea. Thank goodness I had the big caveman with me. I don't think he had a clue what was going on, but somehow he knew I needed his strength and speed to save Galileo. Once we had what we needed, we headed back to the lawn at the Leaning Tower as fast as we could go.

As Bruno and I got closer, we could see a big crowd of professors standing around the acceleration ramp. One man in particular looked very important. He was dressed in purple robes with gold chains. Galileo, Aristotelini, and the

"What is the delay, Galileo?" I heard him complain. "You know better than to keep me waiting."

Aristortelini snickered. "Perhaps he's too embarrassed to admit he's wrong, your Unbelievableness."

"Untrue!" Galileo thundered. "I shall prove before your very eyes that two objects, despite great differences in their weight, will still fall to Earth together."

The crowd laughed out loud. Even the Prince smiled. "I must admit, Galileo, I am quite skeptical. Common sense tells me that a heavier object will always fall faster."

"But that is the beauty of the New Science, Prince," Galileo replied. "By carefully observing experiments, we can discover that nature has an elegance which, sometimes, goes deeper than our own common sense."

"Well, you'll have to show me before I believe you," the Prince replied.

Galileo bowed low, catching Bruno and me out of the corner of his eye. "Yes. Yes. At once. Eh . . . I believe all is now prepared . . ."

I nodded enthusiastically and stepped forward with Bruno. In each hand he held one of my bright ideas—bowling balls! Same size, different weights, and nonmagnetic. The Time Tramp's hint about getting the 'iron out' meant exactly what it said. Get the iron cannonball out of the experiment! Now Aristortelini's lodestones could stay right where they were, since they wouldn't mess up the bowling balls a bit.

I noticed the Crew were all smiling. Curtis gave me a quick thumbs-up. Luckily, Bruno missed it.

"What are those?" the Prince asked as I signaled Bruno to drop them on the ground.

"Cannonballs, your Awesomeness," I replied.

"With holes in them?"

Megan stepped forward. "The holes help you hold them. Makes them easier to load into a cannon. It's the latest design."

The Prince looked confused. "I see," he said slowly.

"And they're much smoother than your average cannonball," Curtis said.

"That's right," Megan said. "It makes for a much nicer demonstration. Galileo wants to make this whole experiment as elegant for you as possible, your Highness."

Smelling a trick, Aristortelini jumped in. "Don't let Galileo use some new-fangled cannon balls, your Incredibleness. Make him use good old iron and lead."

"But there's no difference," I quickly countered, hefting the other ball. "This one's a lot heavier."

The Prince turned to Galileo and Aristortelini who stood side by side. "Very well, Galileo. Begin your experiment. I shall award a gold medal to the one who is right and ridicule the other."

The Prince handed the bowling balls back to me and I walked with Galileo to the starting gate. The big moment had arrived. He took a deep breath and began. "Exalted Prince, distinguished professors . . ." he looked at us, "and, eh . . . welcome guests, today I present to you the first day of the New Science! Behold! The acceleration ramp will start the ball rolling toward ever greater discoveries of nature! Ever deeper insights into the wondrous workings of the world! Ever higher knowledge that . . ."

"Yes, yes," the Prince said, impatiently tapping his foot. "Just get on with it."

"Right," Galileo said. "*Uno . . . due . . . tre!*"

He released the starting gate and let them roll. It went like clockwork. The heavy bowling ball and the light bowling ball picked up speed at the exact same rate and finished neck and neck. When they finally rolled to a stop on the lawn, it was so quiet you could've heard a fly sneeze.

The Prince was the first to find his tongue. "But . . . but can it be true? Is it possible that our common sense has been wrong for so long?" He looked at Galileo. "Do it again!" he commanded.

"At once, My lord."

We reloaded the bowling balls, let them roll, and got the exact same result. The Prince slowly shook his head and smiled. When the other professors saw that his Awesomeness's mind had changed, they quickly switched sides and let out a roar of cheers and applause for Galileo. He had done it! In a very real way, he had changed the world. Only Aristortelini still wanted to argue the point.

"But . . . but that's impossible!" he shouted. "Make him do it again and again and again!"

"No problem," Galileo shouted as I helped him reload the bowling balls for a third demonstration. "The same experiment will produce the same results every time!"

We let the bowling balls roll again and, sure enough, a perfect tie. I guess Aristortelini didn't feel like watching anymore. He scurried away like a rat as the Prince picked up the balls to examine them closely. The rest of the Crew used the moment to join me and Galileo at the starting gate.

"You've done it, Super Crew," he was saying. "I could never have proved my ideas without your help."

"Aw shucks," I said. "Piece of cake."

"And it looks like you don't have to worry about Aristortelini anymore," Curtis said.

"That is correct!" The Prince came up and shook Galileo's hand. "I assure you that no one will interfere with your work again. Meet me in my palace for dinner and tell me all about this New Science of yours. I have plenty of gold to finance your future experiments."

"Thank you, your Most Wonderfulness," Galileo said, bowing low.

The Prince shook his head and smiled. "I never would have guessed it, but reality is just stranger than I ever imagined." He boxed Galileo lightly on the shoulder. "Anyway, good job." He waddled off and left us alone.

Galileo looked at us and smiled. "Super Crew," he said, sounding a little choked up, "I don't know how to thank you enough."

"Well," Megan said, thinking out loud. "You could mail us a painting by Michelangelo. It'll be really valuable by the time it arrives. I'll give you our address."

Galileo reached in his pocket for a feather to write with.

"Don't worry about her," Keisha said. "She's just making a joke."

Megan shook her head. "Joke nothing. I say let's take the KC Express to Florence and pick up some masterpieces cheap."

"And I say let's get back to Kinetic City," I said. "I still gotta get ready for my report tomorrow."

"On what?" Galileo asked.

"On you," I answered.

"C'mon, Crew," Keisha said with a laugh. "It's time to make some tracks through time."

CHAPTER FIFTEEN

A Mammoth Appetite

Now that we had the Galileo case wrapped up, there was only one thing left to do: Get Bruno back home. I didn't figure that should be too hard. We were already in the right place, all we had to do was flash back forty thousand years in time. For that we'd need ALEC and the wormhole again. We said our good-byes to Galileo and made our way back to the woods where we'd hidden the KC Express. Bruno's huge muscles came in handy as we removed all the camouflage netting and stuffed it back in the train.

Then, once we were all in the Control Car and buckled in tight, we fired up ALEC and *gave our command to take us back to Bruno's time. Our computer reeled off the calculations and then shot us through the wormhole. We landed in a meadow and came to a stop when we hit a tree.*

"Hey, we're getting better at this," I said, unbuckling my belt and standing up.

"Yeah," Curtis agreed. "I didn't scream that time."

"Hey, Crew," Keisha said. "Check out Bruno."

I glanced over at the caveman. Before we had even come to a complete stop, he was up and looking out the window. When he recognized his home turf, he let out a long, happy howl and hit the green button by the door. We all hopped out with him.

"Bruno must be psyched to be home, huh?" Megan said.

"I'll say," Curtis agreed. "Look at him sniffing the air."

I was sniffing it, too. Something smelled really good. Bruno and I looked at each other and blinked. The answer hit us both at the same time. "Barbecue!" I shouted.

"*Gunk-gunk!*" Bruno seemed to agree.

The caveman broke into a quick trot down a trail and we did our best to keep up. Usually Keisha's by far the fastest, but this time I kept the lead. I was really hungry. The candy bars I normally use for my quick energy boosts had all been sacrificed for the case.

"Where's he leading us?" Megan shouted from the rear.

"I don't know," I shouted back. "But the barbecue smell's getting stronger. C'mon!"

We soon came to a clearing where we once again saw Bruno's cavemen buddies. Around them sat the cavewomen and lots of little cavekids. They were all hanging out around a huge campfire that was roasting the largest piece of meat I had ever seen. At first I was confused, but then it hit me.

"Wow!" I said in total awe. "An entire mammoth! The backyard barbecuing challenge of a lifetime!"

No one paid attention to me, though. All eyes were focused on Bruno. The entire clan let out shouts of joy as they jumped up to hug him. We stood off to the side for a moment so they could have their happy reunion.

"Hey, look," Megan said with a laugh. "Bruno's teaching everybody how to give high fives."

We all clapped and cheered as our favorite caveman traded high fives with even the smallest of the cavekids.

"Well, Crew," Keisha said proudly. "It looks like our work here is done."

I shook my head. "Oh no, it isn't. They're building the fire too big. I'd better show them how to cook it!"

Before the Crew could stop me, I rushed to the fire and tried to pull a hickory branch from the fire. Bruno looked at me and raised his eyebrows. I tried to explain.

"Careful, Bruno," I said. "You're going to burn it."

"Max!" Megan said. "What are you doing? You're stirring it all up." She coughed as a cloud of smoke billowed out and blew in her face.

Suddenly a gust of wind caught the coals and sent more smoke swirling into the air. I couldn't see anything. I could just hear voices calling my name, over and over.

"Max! Max! Max!"

The voices seemed to float in and out with the wind-blown smoke. I couldn't tell up from down. The smoke kept twisting around me like a blanket. I tried to run but my legs didn't seem to work. The voices calling my name seemed to get louder and more intense.

"Max! Max! Wake up! Max, wake up!"

Wake up?

"Wake up, Max!"

Then, with a jolt, my eyes flew open and there stood Keisha, Megan, and Curtis.

But Bruno was gone. So were all the other cave people. And we weren't outside anymore. We were in the Kitchen Car of the KC Express. Then it hit me. I was awake!

But if that was true, why was there still smoke everywhere?

CHAPTER SIXTEEN

Molto Grazie!

As the dream world faded and the real world took its place, I quickly realized what was going on. The Kitchen Car's smoke alarm had gone off and the Crew came rushing in, looking for the fire. What they found was one of my pizzas burning in the oven and me asleep under the table.

"What are you doing, Max?" Keisha scowled. "Do you want to burn the whole train up?"

"No, I just wanted to show Bruno how to . . ."

"Bruno?" Curtis asked. "Who's that?"

Oops. I guess I wasn't totally awake yet.

"Still a little groggy, Siesta Boy?" Megan smiled.

I looked around the smoky Kitchen Car and tried to get my bearings. "Are we back in the future?"

They all looked at each other and shrugged their shoulders. "Yeah, Max," Keisha said. "That's where we are. Are you okay?"

"Uh huh. I'm okay. I was just having this weird dream, that's all. You were all in it."

"Really? Which one of us was the Tin Man?" Curtis said sarcastically.

"What happened?" Megan asked.

"We saved Galileo's big experiment and rescued the future of science."

Keisha smiled. "Man, Max. Just how bizarre is it inside your head anyway?"

"But . . . but it all seemed so real!" I said.

"Well now that you're back from your time trip," Curtis said, "let me show you guys my latest invention." He pulled a remote control from his pocket and punched a few buttons. A portable stereo came rolling through the door on little tank treads.

"Hey," I said. "The Boom Bot!"

Curtis looked at me. "How did you know that? This is the first time I've taken it out of the Lab Car."

"It saved us from the Inquisition's soldiers," I said. "And from a guy who challenged me to a sword duel."

Curtis looked back at me and grinned. "Boy, Max. That's some imagination you got."

"But . . . but . . . it all seemed so real."

A phone rang. "Hey," Keisha said. "The portable hotline." She unclipped the phone from her belt and held it to her ear. "Kinetic City Super Crew, when you want the facts, we hit the tracks. Keisha speaking."

We couldn't hear who it was, but we could see the puzzled expression spread across Keisha's face. After a couple of seconds, she held out the phone to me. "It's for you."

I grabbed the phone. "Hello?"

"Maximilian!" an excited voice said. "I just want to say once again, *molto grazie!* Many thanks for all your help! Because of you and the Super Crew, the future looks bright for science!"

My eyes were as wide as an owl's as I shouted into the phone. "Who is this? Who is this?" But there was just a click on the other end. And another case closed.

THE END

GET REAL!

This and every adventure of the Kinetic City Super Crew is based on real science. But since this particular adventure takes place inside the somewhat goofy mind of Max, the line between what's real and what's make-believe can get kind of fuzzy. Therefore, in order to keep the fuzziness from collecting in your brain like so much belly-button lint, here's some straightforward scoop on just what's true and what isn't. First the real stuff.

As the Crew discover in the story, Galileo was one of the first to prove that nature has regular laws that we all can learn and understand. As Galileo himself once famously said: "Nature is written in the laws of mathematics." In other words, since the same careful experiment will always get the same result, we can use math to describe what happens. Cool, huh?

Another important point is that Galileo lived in a time before scientists specialized in one particular area. That means he did a lot more cool stuff than we could ever squeeze into Max's dream. Still, the Crew does get some first-hand knowledge of two of his more famous discoveries. The first is the one about the balls going down the ramp. Galileo really did this. He used this simple experiment to prove that falling bodies will accelerate at the same rate, regardless of their weights. (The exceptions are for things with lots of air resistance, like feathers.) Although Galileo himself didn't discover the laws of gravity—Isaac Newton did that later on in the same century—the Italian scientist did establish a solid base of observations for Newton to build on. As Newton himself once famously said: "If I have been allowed to see so far, it is only because I am standing on the shoulders of giants." Almost without doubt, the biggest giant Newton had in mind was Galileo!

The second major discovery the Crew gets a taste of is astronomy. Here Galileo's work is even more famous than his work with the mechanics of motion. By building his very own telescope, Galileo was the first scientist to realize that the Moon was a physical object. That sounds obvious to us, but remember, until Galileo's telescope came along, it was generally believed that only the Earth was made out of stuff you could actually hold in your hand. The Moon and all the planets were thought to be made of a special, mysterious substance available only up in the heavens. Thanks to Galileo, people began to realize that our world is but a single jewel in an amazing and enormous Cosmos.

Galileo was also the first to realize that Jupiter had moons of its own. This was very important because those new moons of Jupiter were important evidence for a new theory for how the Universe works. You see, in Galileo's time, almost everybody believed in the idea that the Earth stood at the the center of the Universe while everything orbited around us. By the time Galileo was an old man, it had become clear to anyone willing to look at the evidence honestly that the old system was finished. In its place would come the theory that Galileo believed in: that the Sun is the center of our solar system and that we orbit around it. Just think, while written history goes back about 5,000 years, only for the last 400 years or so have we known that the Earth was moving in space!

One last little point about Galileo and the Crew concerns the swinging pendulum outside his front door. While it's true Galileo discovered that certain kinds of pendulums can be used to measure time, he almost certainly didn't have one swinging outside his laboratory door. In his day and age, it was common for people to place a symbol or trademark outside their front door to show what kind of work they did. For example, a cobbler might have a big shoe, or a tailor a large pair of scissors, or a barrel maker a big barrel. In the mind of Max, Galileo has a swinging pendulum. Makes sense. (Hey, it's not our fault. Max is just a little goofy, that's all.)

Okay, now that we've gone through the true stuff, let's talk about the story's bizarre twists and turns. First, the wormhole. As any astronomer will tell you, the Universe is an amazing place with lots of stuff that we still don't understand. Do wormholes really exist? Yes. Can four kids in a super train use one to zip back through time? Well, unless some extraterrestrial pops up and shows us how to do it, it's a safe bet it's purely the mind of Max on this one.

So what about Bruno the caveman? Did Neanderthals really exist? They sure did. From studies of their bones, we know that they were in Europe 40,000 years ago. Unfortunately, they didn't leave much behind so we know practically nothing about how they lived. This means that anything you read here about their clothes and customs are all part of Max's imagination.

Home Crew
Hands On

Hey, Home Crew,

Remember that report on Galileo I had to do? As you might imagine, my dream made the whole thing easier. Anyway, here's how it went the very next day at school ...

"I see Maximilian will be next," Ms. Fussmacher said in her unbelievably nasal voice. "Your report's on Galileo, correct?"

I nodded. "Yes, Ms. Fussmacher."

She smiled. "Excellent. I have great expectations for you."

Great. Talk about pressure. All my teachers think that because I'm a member of the KC Express now, I must be some kind of genius. It's not true, of course. I went up to the chalkboard.

"As you just heard," I began, walking up to the front of the room. "My report is on Galileo—the guy who got modern science rolling along."

"Oh," one of the kids in the back said. "So it's that guy's fault, huh?"

"What do you mean?" I asked.

"It's his fault I gotta sit through science class next period."

"And what's wrong with that, Gerald?" Ms. Fussmacher scowled.

The kid shook his head. "It's too hard. We should just have lunch period all day. Or pep rallies. Those are pretty cool, I guess."

I tried to point out why he was wrong. "But think of all the stuff that wouldn't exist if it weren't for science."

He looked skeptical. "Name something."

The challenge caught me off guard. How to pick only one example when there're millions to choose from? "Um . . . television," I said.

He shrugged. "Okay, great. So science figured out TVs. Now that we have them, we can quit learning about it."

Ms. Fussmacher let out a long, slow sigh. I was quickly realizing that teaching can be really frustrating. Still, I thought I could break through the kid's thick mind if I could show him some science in action. I'd use a classroom version of Galileo's acceleration ramp. I'd need some help to set it up.

"Can I get a volunteer to give me a hand?"

"I'll help." That was Ginny, the girl who sits behind me. The butterflies took off in my stomach like a fighter squadron. Don't tell anybody this, but I kinda like her.

"What do we do?" she asked when she came up.

I tapped on the table set up in front of the chalkboard. "We need to tilt this thing a little." I looked at the class. "Can I borrow a couple of textbooks?"

"Here. Take mine," Gerald said. "It's not like I use them a lot anyway."

I quickly lifted the table while Ginny stuck them under the legs. The result was a ramp at a very low angle.

"Okay," I said to the class. "I'm about to race a basketball and a tennis ball down the table. What do you think will happen?"

"They'll fall off the end, dude," Gerald said. His buddies snickered.

"Hah, hah," I said. "I meant which one would finish first?"

"Um, the basketball," he answered. "It's a lot heavier."

I was about to explain why he was wrong, but Ginny jumped in first. "Actually, it should be a tie, right, Max?"

"That's right," I grinned. "All objects fall with the same acceleration, regardless of their mass."

"Huh?" Gerald didn't get it. Most of the rest of the class was confused too. "I don't believe you," Gerald said.

Ginny smiled. "Not only am I sure they'll tie, but I'd bet that both will accelerate at thirty-two feet per second squared if we drop them from the roof of Kinetic City Tower."

Whoa. I knew Ginny was smart, but I had no idea how smart. Brains and beauty. Some people have it all.

"Cool!" Gerald said. He grabbed his board. "Field trip!"

Ms. Fussmacher snapped her fingers to sit him back down.

"Look," I said. "We don't have to go to a roof to prove this. That's the beauty of the acceleration ramp. It slows the fall down so you can see the results. Galileo thought it up himself."

With that, I grabbed the basketball and tennis ball and placed them at the top end of the table. In order to make it as much like Galileo's experiment as possible, I had Ginny hold a yardstick to use as a starting gate.

"Okay, everybody," I called out. "Now keep your eyes on the finish line." I nodded to Ginny. "Let 'em roll."

She pulled the yardstick away and let gravity take its course. Even though the basketball was a lot heavier than the tennis ball, both rolled down the length of the table neck and neck.

"It's a tie!" the whole class called out as both balls fell off the edge at the same time.

"I knew it would be," Ginny said. "Galileo's laws of motion have been the bedrock of science for the last four hundred years."

I shook my head in genuine respect. Ginny could be a member of the Super Crew easy.

So anyway, Home Crew, that's how it went for me. Would things be pretty similar at your school? Why don't you try it? Practice your technique at home first and then ask a teacher for permission to give a classroom demonstration. Who knows? You might get some cool science off and rolling at your own school. (Or at least some extra credit.) If you do the demo, we'd love to know. Call us and tell us about it. We're at 1-800-877-CREW.

Good luck, Home Crew!
Your friend,

Max

Puzzle Pages

Scrambled Message

Ciao, kids! Galileo here with one last problem. It seems after I fired Tony the traitor for his dirty tricks, he tried to send a secret message to the Prince. Luckily my ex-assistant got confused and sent it to me by mistake. Help me decode it in order to learn what Tony was trying to say to the Prince. Here is the letter:

Your Magnificence,

Galileo thinks he's hot stuff because he was one of the first to develop the New $\underset{1\ \ 2\ \ 3}{\_\ \_\ \_\ \_\ \_\ \_\ \_}$. (INECECS) The truth is totally different! *I'm* the one who thought everything up! For example, that $\underset{4\ \ 5}{\_\ \_\ \_\ \_\ \_\ \_\ \_\ \_}$ (LMUUEDPN) swinging in front of his door was my idea. I used

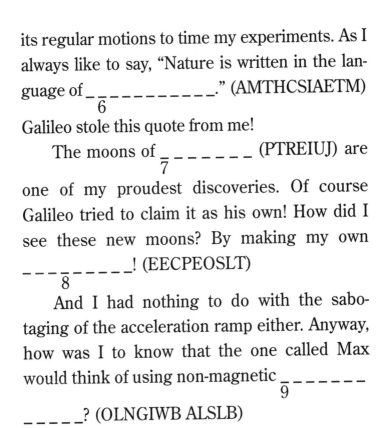

its regular motions to time my experiments. As I always like to say, "Nature is written in the language of _ _ _ _ _ _ _ _ _ _ _." (AMTHCSIAETM)
      6

Galileo stole this quote from me!

The moons of _ _ _ _ _ _ _ (PTREIUJ) are
       7
one of my proudest discoveries. Of course Galileo tried to claim it as his own! How did I see these new moons? By making my own _ _ _ _ _ _ _ _ _! (EECPEOSLT)
    8

And I had nothing to do with the sabotaging of the acceleration ramp either. Anyway, how was I to know that the one called Max would think of using non-magnetic _ _ _ _ _ _ _
              9
_ _ _ _ _? (OLNGIWB ALSLB)

Your Humble Servant,
Tony

Match the lettered numbers here to decode Tony's secret message to the Prince!

$\overline{1}\ \overline{2}\overline{3}\overline{4}\overline{5}\ \overline{6}\ \overline{7}\overline{8}\overline{9}$!

The Long and Short of It

The answers to these questions are all long words. But you can figure them out by coming up with a bunch of short words. Fill in the blanks so that a three-letter word reads down in each column. There may be more than one letter that works for each blank, but only the right one will give you the correct long word answer. Here's an example:

These lived in the areas that are now Europe and western Asia about forty thousand years ago.

A W B A A G A A T M E A
N E A N D E R T H A L S
D T G T D T E E P F H

1. Galileo built a ramp to prove that every falling object does this at the same rate.

   R I A L E P A T A N A

   _ _ _ _ _ _ _ _ _ _ _ _
   T E T G K G T G E T K

2. The cannonballs Galileo used were different weights even though they were the same size. That's because lead and iron have different _____.

   O T E A R A B B U

   _ _ _ _ _ _ _ _ _ _
   D N D K B E T G E

3. This Greek philosopher is one of the greatest minds in history, but Galileo proved he was all wrong when it came to physics.

   W A H A A F A O N

   _ _ _ _ _ _ _ _ _
   G K T H E G E D T

4. Some people thought Galileo was nuts for doing these.

S A A L A Z I L O A A

_ _ _ _ _ _ _ _ _ _ _

T E E T T P P G E E K

Crack the Code

In the following list, there are ten words you might think of when you hear the name Galileo. But they're in code! Every letter of the alphabet has been replaced with a different letter. We've decoded the first word for you. Use these letters in the remaining words and see if you can crack the rest of the code! UGGR SXEA!

1. E K Q Z T K L
   <u>C</u> <u>R</u> <u>A</u> <u>T</u> <u>E</u> <u>R</u> <u>S</u>

2. U K Q C O Z N

   _ _ _ _ _ _ _

3. Q L Z K G F G D N

   _ _ _ _ _ _ _ _ _

4. D G G F

   _ _ _ _

5. Z T S T L E G H T

– – – – – – – – –

6. S Q W G K Q Z G K N

– – – – – – – – – –

7. H T F R X S X D

– – – – – – – –

8. H O L Q

– – – –

9. H I N L O E L

– – – – – – –

10. T B H T K O D T F Z

– – – – – – – – – –

BONUS! Can you guess how we came up with our code?

HINT: We used a computer, but we didn't even have to turn it on!

Answers

Scrambled Message

The scrambled words in the message were:
 science
 pendulum
 mathematics
 Jupiter
 telescope
 bowling balls

 Tony's secret message: I need a job!

The Long and Short of It

 1. accelerates
 2. densities
 3. Aristotle
 4. experiments

Crack the Code

1. craters
2. gravity
3. astronomy
4. moon
5. telescope
6. laboratory
7. pendulum
8. pisa
9. physics
10. experiment

BONUS: Here's the alphabet and corre-sponding code letters:

A B C D E F G H I J K L M N O P Q R S T U V W X Y Z

Q W E R T Y U I O P A S D F G H J K L Z X C V B N M

Now do you see how we did came up with our code?

We used the letters as they appear in the rows of type on a typewriter or computer keyboard.

Anti-Grav Device

You can defy the law of gravity (sort of). You'll need an inflated balloon and a bendable straw, bent into an "L" shape. Put the long end in your mouth with the short end sticking up. Hold the balloon over the end of the straw. Blow a steady stream of air and let go of the balloon. The air pushing against the balloon should be enough to resist gravity's pull. See how long you can keep the balloon floating in mid-air.

SuperCrew
instant ideas
just add brain power and stir

Playground Pendulum

The next time you're at a playground, grab an empty swing and pull it back to a specific spot. Then let go (don't push it) and count the number of swings in ten seconds. Then have a friend sit in the swing. Pull you friend back to the same spot and let go. Again, count the number of swings in ten seconds. What do you think will happen? Here's a hint: A swing doesn't do its thing without gravity.

Other Case Files

From Truffle Trouble
The Case of the Fungus among Us

It had been pretty smart of Mr. Cloulez to hide in the treetops when Madame Lafinque was trying to find him. But it wasn't smart of him at all to get stuck—especially now that a bunch of angry people were making their way in our direction. PJ shimmied up the tree and started untying Mr. Cloulez's shoelace. Derek, Max, and I braced ourselves for their arrival. As they got closer, we heard them chanting "VA T'EN, CLAUDE CLOULEZ!" . . .

"What are they saying?" Max asked.

"Go away, Claude Cloulez," Derek told him.

"They're carrying torches!" Max exclaimed.

"Those are flashlights, Max," Derek said.

The mob reached the top of the driveway where we were standing, and came to a stop. All told, there were probably two or three dozen people. One of the men in front addressed us in English.

"We have come to chase Claude Cloulez out of town," he said angrily. "Step aside!"

The mob roared in agreement.

"It was bad enough when the curse interfered with our crops and our health. But when you brought the curse into the bistro today, you ruined my lunch! That I cannot accept!"

"Don't you know there's no such thing as a curse?" Derek asked in his usual stubborn fashion.

"Not true," said an old woman. "We have recorded the suffering caused by this family for hundreds of years: The Fire of 1798. The Avalanche of 1836. The chronic heartburn epidemic of 1978!"

"Are you sure the Cloulez family was responsible for those things?" Derek asked.

"Absolutely," said a young man. "Things were fine the last few years with no Cloulez people around. But the day Mr. Cloulez returned, my girlfriend broke up with me! And I was diagnosed with incurable bad breath!"

The crowd murmured in horror and sympathy.

"Hmm," Derek said thoughtfully. "Don't you think she broke up with you because of your breath?"

"What are you saying?" the young man shouted. "That is ridiculous! The Cloulez curse is the source of all our woes!"

The crowd rumbled with anger again.

"You can't reason with them, Derek," Max said under

his breath.

"He's right," I whispered.

"Tell us where Cloulez is," the first man said. "That's all we want to know."

I was about to invite the mob to look for Mr. Cloulez in the house, since it was now completely dark and both he and PJ were safely out of sight up in the tree. But just then, PJ or Mr. Cloulez slipped, and a small branch broke off and fell to the ground.

Immediately, the group shined their flashlights into the tree. PJ and Mr. Cloulez were hanging in the branches like a pair of frightened raccoons.

"There he is! Get him!" the young man cried. The crowd rushed to surround the base of the tree.

———⟫◆⟪———

From U.F. uh-Oh:
The Case of the Mayor's Martians

We all hopped in the Desert Rover and sped around to the other side of Mount Squashmore. It took longer than I thought. Between Area 15 and the mountain itself, there was a lot to circle around. The sand flying in our faces didn't make it any easier. But I felt like I had to see what those "flying saucers" really were.

I didn't really know what to expect. After that weird tour and the slimy goo in the closet, some part of my mind couldn't help thinking that the alien story might just be real. Or at least that something creepy was going on. But the no-nonsense, scientific part told me not to jump to conclusions. I guess both parts really wanted to see what this thing was.

As it turned out, neither of them would get the chance. When we finally turned the corner behind the mountain, we saw a couple of familiar faces. It was Lars and Louie, the guys in the dark suits and sunglasses who had towed Stacy back to Kinetic City. This time, they were in a different truck. It looked like a moving van, except it was *black like the tow truck. And it looked like they had just packed away whatever had landed back there . . .*

"Excuse me!" Keisha firmly but politely called out to the agents. "Lars? Louie? It's us, the Kinetic City Super Crew." She flashed her Super Crew ID card just to keep it legit.

"That's right," Megan said. "We're the Mayor's special guests, remember?"

"No," said Lars in his flattest monotone.

"Don't be silly, Lars," Louie said. He turned to us. "He's a kidder, Lars is. Great sense of humor." Lars just stared straight ahead with a steely scowl. "Of course we remember you. How was your tour, folks?"

"Very enlightening," Mr. Snerr said. "But the best part was the end. We saw some flying saucers land in this very spot!"

"What?" Louie asked. Lars frowned.

"What he means is, did anything just land out here?" I explained. "Something metal? On a parachute?"

"No," Lars replied firmly.

"That's right!" Louie added. "Nothing's landed back here since, well . . . I can't remember, because it probably never happened!"

"Quiet, Louie," Lars snarled.

"No, really," Fernando insisted. "We just saw something come out of the sky. It should have landed right around here."

I felt like being bold. "You're not hiding it, are you?"

"No," said Lars.

"Absolutely not!" Louie chimed in. "If you saw something, it was probably really boring. Even if something did land out here, and we had it in the truck right now, you wouldn't want to look at it."

"Actually, we kinda would," Megan said. "Can we take a peek?"

"No," said Lars.

"That's right! There's no reason to look in the truck," Louie chirped. "We just happened to be driving by here. This metal thing that's in our truck right now has nothing to do with the thing you saw. Or the Mayor. Or some secret of his. Or aliens."

"Wait a second. We didn't mention the Mayor. Or some secret of his. Or aliens," I said suspiciously.

"And you just said you had something metal in the truck," Snerr noted.

Lars flashed Louie a glare that would melt concrete. "Get in the truck, Louie," he said. Louie nodded in agreement.

He looked like he'd said enough. "Sure thing, boss." He turned to us. "Remember, this was all very, very boring!" He climbed into the passenger seat. Lars revved up the engine and they sped away, around the other side of the mountain.

"That's it! I'm going after them!" Keisha said. She hopped into the Desert Rover and cranked the ignition.

"I'll come with you!" Fernando said. "You three stay here and look for evidence!"

"Roger that!" I said. Fernando hopped in the dune buggy's passenger seat. Then Keisha hit the accelerator, and the two of them sped off.

—————⟫◆⟪—————

From Home Run Has Been
The Case of the Sluggish Slugger

"Kinetic City Super Crew," I said, picking up the phone. "When you want the facts—"

"Megan, this is Rudy Derosa. And yes, I'd like some facts."

"Hi, Mr. Derosa," I said. "What's up?" I tried to sound cool, but in truth I felt pretty nervous. We'd never been so far from solving a case with so little time left.

"I can't believe you told the press before you told me," he said.

"Told them what?" I asked, surprised by the question. As far as I could remember, all we'd said to the press was a whole heap of "no comments."

"Told them about Boomer cheating!" Mr. Derosa replied angrily.

"What?" I asked. "We didn't say that!" I looked anxiously at the rest of the Crew. They could tell something alarming was going on.

"Maybe you'll remember when I quote you," Mr. Derosa said. "Here it is. The front page of the Kinetic City Gazette. In a headline, no less. " 'SUPER CREW SAYS BOOMER'S THROWING THE GAMES!' "

For a moment I was stunned silent. "But we—"

"Listen, I can't talk anymore," Mr. Derosa said. "Sally Frost is waiting to see me. I think she wants to kill me."

"Why? What did you do?" I asked.

"What did I do? I told Boomer I was going to fire him!" Mr. Derosa said. "He was cheating!"

"No he wasn't! I mean, maybe he was, but we don't..." My mind was racing too fast to talk straight. "You can't do that yet. We don't have any proof!" I blurted.

"What did you say?" Mr. Derosa asked.

"The paper misquoted us," I said. "We, I mean I, thought he might be cheating, but we don't know that for sure."

"I think you'd better get down here, quick," Mr. Derosa said. "If we don't straighten this out soon, there's going to be a riot. This place is filling up with some angry fans. Reporters are everywhere. Sally Frost is on the warpath, and Boomer's packing up his gear for good!"

"We'll be right there," I said. I hung up the phone and slumped into a chair.

The rest of the Crew was beside themselves.

"What is it, Megan?"

"What's going on?"

"What happened?"

I looked at them blankly. "Oops," I said.

From Tall Tales:
The Case of the Growing Suspicions

I checked both Patsy and Brent to make sure they were quiet, then carefully stepped over toward the cooler. This was it—my big moment. Ever so slowly, I lifted the cover of the cooler. But the hinges were totally creaky! No matter how slowly I lifted, it still made tons of noise. I could practically hear the rest of the Crew cringe. I waited a moment, then opened it a little further. It creaked some more.

"Hey, hey, hey," Brent muttered. I was sure I was caught then, but when I glanced over I noticed that his eyes were still shut. I opened the cooler the last few inches and reached inside.

"I'm a hunk AND I'm going to be famous," Brent said in his sleep.

This wasn't good. He seemed too restless. I grabbed a bottle from inside the cooler and brought it up to my face. The growth potion! Score! I was so excited I almost shouted at the rest of the Crew. But this was no time to lose my cool. I slid the bottle in my pocket. Then, ever so carefully, I lowered the cover of the cooler, and crept away.

Mr. Grrow and the rest of the Crew were crouched on the other side of the campfire. "Got it," I whispered when I reached them.

"Good job, Megan," they said. "Now we need to get out of here."

"Wait ONE second," Mr. Grrow said, getting down on the ground. "I think I dropped the keys to my helicopter."

"Oh no," Max said. "We have to get out of here."

"Oh, here they are," Mr. Grrow said, scooping up the keys from the ground.

We breathed a sigh of relief. We were safe!

Just then, a voice broke through the darkness.

"Hey, who's there?!" Brent growled.

"Uh oh," Max said, as we froze in our tracks. "We're in for it now."

———⟫◆⟪———

From **Forest Slump:**
The Case of the Pilfered Pine Needles

There we were in the darkest forest we'd ever been in, looking for who-knows-what to appear . . .

"Hey," Keisha said. "Where *is* Max?"

"I didn't see him, did you, Curtis?" I asked.

He shook his head. "Has anyone been listening to their walkie-talkies since we left the trees?"

"Uh–oh," Keisha said nervously.

Curtis pulled the antenna up on his walkie-talkie and switched it on.

"I said HELP!!!!" Max's voice wailed over the line.

"Max!" Curtis said. "Is this for real?"

"AHHHHH!" was all Max said. A strange crashing sound and a rumble followed, and then there was silence.

. . . Who would have guessed that we'd get into so much trouble by investigating something as harmless sounding as pine needles?!

———⟫◆⟪———

NOW HEAR THIS!!

Tune in to the
Kinetic City Super Crew
radio show every week!

If you think reading about the Crew is cool,
wait till you hear them blasting out of your radio.
Every week the Super Crew find themselves tangled up
in danger and mystery in a different place...
from the icy tundras of Alaska to the busy
streets of Kinetic City.

Call 1-800-877-CREW (2739)
to find out where you can tune in to hear
the next awesome episode of
Kinetic City Super Crew.

KCSC is featured on finer
public radio stations around the country.

 AMERICAN ASSOCIATION FOR THE
ADVANCEMENT OF SCIENCE

National Science Foundation

```
Check out
Kinetic City Cyber Club
a science mystery game
on the World Wide Web
```

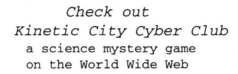

Come and Play!
http://www.kineticcity.com

How would you like to try solving your own mystery with the Super Crew? It's waiting for you now, at Kineticcity.com!

You'll also find games, info on your favorite Super Crew members, online chats, and cool things to download, like stationery and screen savers. There's even a page for teachers and parents.

When you get to the site make sure you bookmark it. You'll want to go there every day because there's always something new and fun happening at Kinetic City Cyber Club!

AMERICAN ASSOCIATION FOR THE
ADVANCEMENT OF SCIENCE

National Science Foundation